Nursery Crimes

Nursery Crimes

B. M. Gill

CHARLES SCRIBNER'S SONS / NEW YORK

This novel is a work of fiction. Names, characters, places, and incidents either are the product of the author's imagination or are used fictitiously. Any resemblance to actual events or persons, living or dead, is entirely coincidental.

Library of Congress Cataloging-in-Publication Data

Gill, B. M.
  Nursery crimes.

  I. Title.
PR6057.I538N8   1987   823'.914   86-29776
ISBN 0-684-18800-7

Manufactured by The Haddon Craftsmen, Inc., Scranton, Pennsylvania

First American Edition 1987

Nursery Crimes

One

When she was quite sure that Willie was dead Zanny began to scream. She screamed shrilly and with all her might. In all her six years she had never screamed so loud. Even the goldfish were scared. They swam around Willie's submerged yellow head like aquatic dancers caught off-beat. One frantically nibbled the lobe of Willie's ear before Zanny pushed it away with the toe of her sandal.

She climbed out of the goldfish pond, wet to the armpits, and roared lustily once more, her face up-turned to the sky. Spitfires returning to base waggled a victory roll as they burst through cream cumulus, their engines making a staccato racket as if noise were released in small explosive quantities. Temporarily silenced, Zanny watched the squadron depart. Daddy flew aeroplanes, too. Bigger than those. Daddy flew bombers.

She began screaming again. For Mummy.

Clare Moncrief was in bed with the local doctor when Zanny's screams shattered the post-coital calm.

Usually she and Peter made love when Zanny and the two little evacuees from Birmingham – Dolly and her brother, Willie – were off the premises in the infants school down in the village. But today was a holiday and the children were spending the morning in the garden, playing peacefully. Until now.

"It seems," she said, hurriedly pulling on her clothes, "that my daughter needs me."

"Rather urgently," Doctor Tolliston agreed, suppressing his annoyance. He had three children of his own

7

and knew how to interpret the varying degrees of vocalised distress.

He was the first to arrive at the goldfish pond, but Clare was the first to look in.

"Dear God!" she gasped.

Later that day Graham Moncrief arranged compassionate leave from his air base and arrived home in Wales at seven o'clock. Zanny heard him going into Dolly's bedroom and then, after spending some time with her, he came into hers.

She was delighted to see him. "Hi, Daddy!"

"Hi, Zanny!"

He kissed her and she twined her arms around him and hugged him.

"Mummy said you were coming. I stayed awake specially. You shouldn't have gone to see Dolly first. I love you. Love you. Love you!"

Graham released himself gently and sat beside her on the bed. How in hell, he wondered, was he to broach this most appalling subject and keep relatively calm? The knowledge that Clare, sick with worry, was waiting downstairs while he tried to find the truth of the horrendous business, didn't help. The truth might not be desirable. Quite the reverse. So why seek it? But he must.

"Dolly is very sad about her brother's accident, darling. We all are." He did a little careful probing. "When little boys of four fall into ponds – shallow ponds – they usually get out again. I wonder why Willie didn't?"

Zanny arranged her pillow more comfortably and didn't answer.

"Don't you know, sweetheart?"

She smiled and shook her head.

He tried the oblique approach. "I see that Monkey has crept back into your bed." The cuddly toy had been given to Willie, he remembered, as a forcible peace

8

offering after Willie had poked his tongue out at Zanny and she had retaliated by jabbing her finger in his eye.

"You must be kind to your little guests," Clare had said, sounding impossibly prissy.

"Bugger!" Zanny had replied, "and I learnt it from him."

Zanny rubbed Monkey's ear up and down her cheek. Monkey was hers again now. For ever. She said she had fetched it from Willie's bed.

"Willie won't be sleeping there any more, Zanny."

"No," Zanny agreed happily. "His body will be put in a box – like Mick. And his soul will go to Jesus – like Mick." Mick, the labrador, had died of old age six months ago. She asked her father if Willie would be buried in the garden.

At that point Graham nearly lost his cool and it was a moment or two before he could answer. He told her that only animals and birds were buried in the garden and that Willie would be buried in a cemetery.

"With his Mummy and Daddy?"

Graham said yes. Willie's parents had been killed in an air-raid and you didn't bury bits, but you didn't harass your six-year-old daughter with that kind of information.

Zanny chewed Monkey's toe. It was a beautiful long toe like a hand. When she had caught Willie chewing it she had pushed it down his throat and then withdrawn it quickly before he was sick.

"That's all right then," she said.

"What is, Zanny?"

"Willie will have his Mummy and Daddy – and Jesus – and Mick."

"Well – yes – but – " Graham got up from the bed and began roaming around the room. He had slept in this same room when he was a boy. There should be something comforting about the place. The walls should be steeped in normal happy memories. His father had beaten him here once at the age of ten for drinking an

9

illicit whisky. Sane – occasionally painful – pre-war days. No evacuees. No Willie.

No beloved daughter with honey curls and eyes as serenely blue as the summer evening sky.

Oh, Christ.

"Darling, you did like Willie, didn't you?"

The clouding of the serenely blue eyes answered him. He interrupted the truth before the lips formed it.

"Well, of course you did. He was a nice little boy. Awkward at times – you quarrelled at times – well, naturally. But you liked him. You liked him like you would a brother."

He went and sat on the bed again and took her hand in his. A ridiculously small hand, though Willie's had been smaller.

"You know what policemen are, don't you, darling?"

"Good, kind men who tell you the time and find you when you're lost," Zanny parroted.

Graham stroked her hand. "And ask questions about little boys who run too fast and fall into goldfish ponds." He looked closely at her – and wished he hadn't. She couldn't dissimulate. She didn't even try.

"Zanny," he spoke urgently, "when the good, kind policeman comes here tomorrow and asks you questions about Willie you won't tell him anything silly, will you?"

"No, Daddy, of course not."

"Remember you liked him very much. You didn't push him – or anything. You are very sad about the accident. You did your best to get him out of the pond, but you couldn't."

The fact that Willie was small for his age, and frail, was something the police might not think about. Anyway, Zanny hadn't been expected to *save* him.

It seemed wise to leave it at that. Well, there was nothing more he could do, damn it!

He settled her down for the night, kissed her, and then, because she told him to, he kissed Monkey as well.

Once downstairs, tasting wet fur, Graham went straight over to the drinks cabinet and poured himself a liberal measure of scotch.

Clare, red-eyed from weeping, was nursing a gin and tonic. She was afraid to hear the answer, but the question had to be asked. "Well, Graham – did she?"

He avoided a direct reply and said it was fortunate that Willie's parents weren't around to make trouble.

Clare pointed out that his grandmother was and would be coming the following day. "In God's name, what do we tell her?"

"The truth."

Her teeth were chattering against the glass. "Which truth?"

"The only sensible truth. Willie fell in. Banged his head. Died. Zanny ran to help. Got scared. Began to holler."

He suddenly remembered Tolliston. In this context infidelity was a minor peccadillo. "If Tolliston shops Zanny at the inquest, I'll shop him. For professional misconduct with a patient. As from now, you'll cool it."

This wasn't the time to deny anything. He wouldn't believe her, anyway. "Then you really think that Zanny . . .?"

They felt sudden compassion for each other – a need to touch. He put his glass down cn the mantelpiece and rubbed the skin along the line of her jaw.

"You told the police it was an accident. Tomorrow Zanny will tell them it was an accident. That's what we think – that it was an accident.'

"Yes," she agreed, "that's what we think." To herself she amended it. "That's what we think when we think out loud."

It had been a terrible day. The police had asked a lot of questions, but hadn't persisted when Peter had blocked their path to Zanny and urged them to let the child be until the following day.

"She's a baby of six," he had said, "and badly shocked. As the family's physician I must insist that she has a night's rest before being questioned." He had been a buttress of strength until Graham had arrived. And then he had tactfully withdrawn.

Graham's finger along her jaw was very soothing. It occurred to her that under different circumstances an undefended accusation about Peter would have resulted in a bruised jaw rather than a caressed one. Not that he was a man of violence, but given cause . . .

Not that Zanny was a violent child, but given cause . . .

She loved Monkey very much. It had been unwise to give her prized possession to Willie. Even as a well-deserved peace offering.

"Monkey," Graham said, picking up her thought, "is back in Zanny's arms. Dolly, when I went in to see her, was nursing the revolting Miranda and wiping her nose in its hair." He had given her a handkerchief and told her gently how very sorry he was. Dolly's eyes and nose tended to run even when there was no great cause for grief. Now that there was cause he sensed that the tears were perfunctory rather than real. She hadn't liked her little brother very much. He was her possession, however, and that possession had been forcibly removed. The equation was obvious. With Monkey and Willie now on the minus side, Dolly was outraged. Quietly, politely outraged.

"You saw him fall?" he had anxiously probed.

Dolly had made a slight movement of her head which might have gone either way.

"Yes or no?" he had insisted.

Her eyes were brown liquid caverns – her only good feature. They were clearly asking him what response he wanted; that she would say anything to oblige. "Ta, very much," she had a habit of saying. For clean sheets. For a breakfast egg. For a bandage on a cut knee. And once, with a degree of unchildlike sarcasm, for a slap –

12

from Zanny, of course. No one else had ever touched her in wrath, not even in exasperation. Clare had kissed her and Willie on any occasion on which a kiss had appeared necessary – a polite salutation which Willie had invariably rubbed off crossly and which Dolly had politely put up with. Neither child had ever kissed anybody back. The second shake of the head was more definitely negative and had calmed him.

"Poor little Dolly," Clare said. "Do you think I ought to go up and cuddle her?"

"No," Graham said crisply. He understood the parental bond. And he understood its absence. Some surrogate parents and some evacuees crossed boundaries and it worked. But here it didn't. Clare was conscientious. Clare was fair. Clare, in this respect like Dolly, was polite. The children's underwear had been removed discreetly and burnt. Fresh clothing, including pretty nightwear, had been provided. Clothing coupons had limited quantity, but Clare had been generous as regards quality. The children, skinny on arrival, had begun to thrive physically. Here in the hills of Merionethshire they could hear the German planes on their way to bomb the northern cities, but bombs were rarely wasted en route. They slept at night with a degree of peace. Two little evacuees were Clare's contribution to the beating of Hitler. Graham meted out carnage for carnage. She blew noses and wiped bottoms and de-nitted. There was no great passion about any of it. The passion was Zanny's. The capacity for hatred was deep in Zanny. But then so was the capacity to love.

She was crooning gently to Monkey and rocking him in her arms when she felt the bedclothes being pulled back in the dark and Dolly getting in beside her.

Here was menace.

Here was change.

Dolly had never got into her bed before. If she had, she would have thrown her out. Her legs were longer than Zanny's and she pushed the metal hot-water bottle away from Zanny's side of the bed and appropriated it. Zanny, enraged but wary, held Monkey close. Dolly smelt of camphorated oil. Mummy had rubbed it on her chest the other night. She hadn't rubbed it tonight. Tonight Willie was dead and ordinary things were forgotten. Even baths.

Dolly, warm with the bottle, settled herself comfortably and began choosing her words with some care.

"They 'ang you," she said, "and then they slits your stommack – and last of all they takes your 'ead off and puts it on a spike." She smiled sweetly in the darkness. British history, when it occasionally strayed into the curriculum of a seven-year-old, tended to be dull. In the playground the older children were more enlightening.

Zanny put Monkey's thumb in her mouth and sucked it contemplatively. She was following the gist very well – apart from ang. What was ang? And who were they?

She took Monkey's thumb out. Her stomach felt raw and her head felt funny. She asked distantly and coldly what ang was.

Dolly proceeded to enlighten her with some joy. "They puts this rope around your neck, see, and they stands you on a chair – and then they kicks the chair – and the rope gets tight – squeech – squeech – squeech – tight – tight – tight – and your eyes drop out of your bleedin' 'ead." Then she added for good measure, "On a plate – like two fried eggs."

Zanny digested this piece of information after some rising of bile and a desire to vomit.

"And who," she ventured to ask, "are they?"

"Dear, good, kind perlicemen," said Dolly. Some of Clare's indoctrination had taken effect. A few weeks ago she would have described them differently. Their function here and back home in Birmingham would, however, be the same. Murder, wherever it happened, was murder.

Zanny lay as still as a board, Monkey pressed tight against her chest. It was perfectly obvious that Dolly in

14

her nasty spying way had been lurking somewhere in the bushes and had seen the fight, the push, the splash, the struggle, the final victory. She had wondered why she had been hustled away from the pool so fast. That anyone, particularly dear, kind policemen, should take any interest filled her with surprise.

She had also been aware that Daddy's talk with her hadn't been as simple as it seemed. He had been trying to force some words into her head and push other words out. Like a school performance of the Knave of Hearts. "Oh dear, wherever are my tarts?" was the line she had to learn then. "I've lost me bleedin' buns," had been Dolly's prompt from the wings. Disdain for Dolly's superior memory had kept her silent. Dolly, normally so self-effacing, had caught the teacher's attention more than once. A surprising infant, Miss Williams had called her. Sharp as a needle.

Surprising, indeed.

Sharp, indeed.

I drowned Willie, Zanny thought, but I can't drown you. You're too big. She had been wondering for some time how to dispose of Dolly. A pillow on her face might do – later on tonight, perhaps, when she was asleep. She smoothed Monkey's ears whilst giving it deep thought.

The urgency of getting rid of Dolly was making her sweat. If she didn't finish her off tonight she would tell the dear, kind policeman things that he shouldn't be told and the dear, kind policeman would do unspeakable things to her like shoving her head on the railings by the front gate.

"Murder," said Dolly complacently, "is a sin."

"What's a sin?"

"Things that make Jesus sad."

This was sufficiently an anti-climax to calm Zanny a little. Jesus being sad didn't worry her very much.

"Scared, aren't you?" Dolly asked, her lips close to Zanny's right ear. Zanny turned her head away.

"Shakin' like a jelly, aren't you?" Dolly persisted,

ignoring the fact that Zanny was rigid with controlled terror.

"You smell," Zanny retorted with some spirit.

"Of your ma's comfray oil. I aint wet meself. I aint wet meself for days."

"You've ruined one mattress," Zanny said in a fair imitation of Mummy when Mummy had believed herself out of earshot. "And mattresses," she went on, "don't grow on trees."

The vision this created held them both silent for a moment or two. "They 'ang you from trees," Dolly said at last, moulding the conversation the way she wanted it.

Zanny suddenly realised what ang meant. She said with deep sarcasm. "Hang. Huh – huh – huh. Huh – *hang. Apples h*ang from trees. Conkers *h*ang from trees."

"Little girls do, too," Dolly said inexorably.

She cuddled closer to Zanny. "You're fat – Zanny Fatty. No wonder little Willie drownded. You put your fat bum on 'is 'ead."

"Bum," Zanny said, denying nothing because it was useless to deny it, "is rude."

"Better'n bein' dead."

This was incontrovertible.

Zanny for the first time in her life imagined herself being dead. Horribly mutilated and dead. Dead as a pig's head on a butcher's slab. With an apple in its mouth. Why did they put apples in pigs' mouths? Why not balls – or wooden tops – or Christmas bells? If they put something in her mouth, what would they put? Despite her fear, sleep was buzzing in her head like a bluebottle.

"Your doll's pram will do," Dolly said.

That was daft. In Dolly's language – plain, bleedin' daft. They'd have to unhinge her jaw for a start. It was a big pram with a hood.

"It would never go in," she said.

16

"In where?"

"My mouth."

Dolly, intent on grabbing Zanny back from the portals of sleep, jabbed her in the ribs.

"It's my mouth we're talkin' about," she said fiercely. "Keepin' it shut. I don't want to eat your bloomin' pram." She giggled. "Soft, aren't you – funny in the 'ead – silly Zanny. You gimme your pram and I won't say nothin' to the nice, kind perliceman tomorrer."

Zanny spiralling down into sleep clung on to what seemed a golden, gauzy promise of reprieve. It was better to have one's stomach and one's head and one's neck than to have a beautiful doll's perambulator. Let Dolly have it. She didn't care. Well, not much. In any case she wouldn't have it for long.

"All right," she agreed.

Dolly, overjoyed, leaned over and kissed her. "Thank you very much, Zanny. Thank you very much indeed." It was a parody of Mummy, not intended, but clearly and very distinctly Mummy.

Zanny, disconcerted, wiped off the kiss.

Willie had wiped off kisses.

Willie in a box a long way away.

Willie swinging from an apple tree in heaven. Picking apples for Jesus.

Goodbye, Willie.

Zanny pushed Monkey's thumb in her mouth and slept.

The next morning Daddy appeared at breakfast in his uniform. Zanny liked his Squadron Leader uniform very much, but Daddy on his rare periods of leave got out of it in double quick time and slouched around in corduroy trousers and a jersey. Zanny sensed that Daddy didn't like the war as much as Mummy liked the war, not that Mummy ever said she liked it, she just glowed quietly and smiled secretly even though her back kept on hurting and her doctor friend had to keep on coming to make it better. The fact that it didn't hurt when Daddy was there was puzzling. Perhaps Daddy knew how to make it better, too. He was a wonderful, kind, nice Daddy. Zanny, a finger of toast in her hand, smiled lovingly at him across the breakfast table.

Oh, God, Graham groaned, looking at her. When a beloved kitten suddenly developed tiger tendencies what could you do? Produce a gun? He and Clare had discussed strategy for several hours during the night. The sexual act, normally long drawn out and pleasurable, had been concluded in a matter of minutes. The spectre of Tolliston might have hovered briefly in the wings, but the drama in the centre of the stage was almost wholly to blame.

Zanny was one hell of a problem.

You coupled. You produced a child. All yellow curls and sweetness. And then she went and did this to you – or more accurately, she did it to little Willie.

He asked Clare if Zanny had shown any violent tendencies before Willie and Dolly had arrived. Clare, who up until now had muffled the truth, much as black-out curtains muffled the light, allowed it to be stated clearly so that all the dangers were revealed.

"On her fifth birthday party she stuck a fork into Jean Thompson because Jean blew out the candles on her cake. She had to have three stitches." She sensed that Graham was grinning in the darkness. "All right – Jean is an odious child and her parents are worse – but she's got a scar and it shows."

She went on to recount several other episodes, the last of which had involved shoving eight-year-old Marjorie's finger into the mangle because she had eaten all of Zanny's sweet ration.

It was all very normal. That was the sort of thing that children did. But they stopped short of murder. Perhaps by the grace of God? Perhaps Zanny was just unlucky. Just that much too strong. Willie that much too weak.

"The common denominator, as I see it," Graham said,

18

"is that Zanny was dispossessed of a monkey. Of the blowing out of candles. Of sweets. She's got her bloody monkey back – make sure that everything of Zanny's remains Zanny's. And get Dolly packed back to Birmingham."

Clare had argued that it was her moral duty to have evacuees and that if Dolly went more would be billeted on her. "And what can I say in refusal? That my daughter is going to pick them off one by one?"

The truth, they both agreed, whilst an effective deterrent to the appalling nuisance of having strangers' children around the place, was better left unsaid. Silence and vigilance were the order of the day.

Detective Inspector Humphreys and Sergeant Pritchard arrived at eleven o'clock. Their elderly Austin Seven wound its way up the drive with a degree of reluctance and much belching of exhaust fumes. Zanny, used to seeing the sergeant on his bike, believed he had been promoted to four wheels on her account and felt a glow of pride. Mummy, who was brushing her hair prior to putting pink ribbons in it, said something under her breath that Zanny didn't hear, and then she knotted the ribbons hastily and crookedly and patted Zanny on the cheek.

The child, Clare thought, looked lovely.

Dolly didn't look too bad either. Her ribbon was a dark blue and she had had more time with it.

As she had groomed the two little girls for the interview she had brainwashed them to the best of her ability. Brainwashing was Graham's name for it and new to her. But it was apt. It fitted. She hoped it worked. Accident, she kept saying – accident – accident.

Graham ushered the two policemen into the living room after the bell had rung a couple of times and it had occurred to him that it was up to him to answer it. Sarah, the maid, had just taken a job in the munitions factory where the wages were somewhat better. The war had caused domestic disruptions and social change which took a little getting used to.

He indicated the chintz-covered sofa in the window recess and told them politely to sit. An offer of a drink came next. They declined.

The three uniformed men looked at each other in silence for several moments. That he belonged to the community gave Graham a certain feeling of ease. His father, grandfather and great-grandfather had lived in the village and though that didn't qualify for total acceptance (their roots, way back in time, were in Northumberland not Wales) it certainly helped. Having owned this house for two generations helped, too. Families, like ancient monuments, became part of the scenery. One didn't kick the foundations.

Graham launched into his prepared speech of regret and then went on to embellish it with tales of little Willie's wildness. The slums of Birmingham, he implied, especially in war-time, bred a toughness of spirit even in a four-year-old. He had been used to freedom and having his own way. He couldn't be watched constantly. He catalogued all the minor accidents that Willie had survived and then went on to speak of the major one that he hadn't. It was a difficult thesis to conclude – that little Willie, little desperado Willie, had swaggered through bomb-torn Birmingham and emerged whole only to drown himself in two feet of water in a goldfish pond in Wales – but he had to try.

"He ran in at some speed, fell and struck his head hard." Graham raised his voice a little, noticing Zanny at the door. "As my daughter will tell you."

Both the police officers rose as Clare came into the room flanked by the two little girls. Sam Humphreys, despite a lifetime of police work, had a streak of sentimentality and thought the trio quite the prettiest picture he had seen for a long time. Mrs. Moncrief with her shoulder length brown hair wore a dress of Madonna blue which exactly matched her eyes – her questioning, anxious, troubled eyes. Her child, Susannah, plump and pretty in pink with matching bows, stood gravely at her side. The other child, not prepossessing, but clean and neat and obviously cared for with Christian charity, was on her right. British motherhood, Sam thought, at its finest and most beautiful. At this particular moment it couldn't even be bettered by Welsh motherhood, and that was saying a great deal.

Sergeant Pritchard, also man enough to be impressed, mentally congratulated Peter Tolliston on making hay in this particular pasture and wondered if Squadron Leader Moncrief knew. He felt a touch of sympathy for him. Hell of a war, this. You metamorphosed yourself from a likeable lad with a degree in accountancy into an airman with a flashy uniform (why was he wearing it now?) who would deal out death and destruction while your wife cuckolded you and your evacuee got drowned. He imagined – quite accurately – what Clare Moncrief was doing while Willie Morton had met his end and his sympathy for her husband grew. He had sired a nice kid there. No doubt about the paternity, at least.

He smiled at Zanny.

Zanny, relieved, smiled back.

Graham, who regarded Dolly as an unpredictable time-bomb, had toyed with the idea of not having her present at the interview. But the police would probably want to talk to her anyway and on balance it was better to have her as one of a group and within earshot. God knows what she might say in a private interrogation.

Interrogation?

What rubbish!

A gentle talk to a couple of babies.

He realised he had begun to sweat.

Sam Humphreys took a bag of toffees out of his pocket. "Hello, Susannah," he said, "would you like a sweetie?"

Zanny, torn between desire and a deep and almost adult knowledge that she must tread with a great deal of care and always say the right thing, hesitated. Bad men gave children sweets. They were bad men because you didn't know them. She didn't know this man. He had white hair and he was very old. His jaws sagged. Sergeant Pritchard was a good man. He rode a bicycle and waved when he saw her out for a walk. Had he proffered her a sweet she would have taken one.

"No, thank you," she said.

The inspector, surprised, offered the bag to the other child.

"Ta," said Dolly, taking two, "ta very much."

The preliminaries over, Humphreys went to sit again. He looked consideringly at Zanny. Zanny, aware that he would have liked her better had she taken a sweet and intensely jealous that Dolly had two and was chewing away with greedy enjoyment, looked back at him cautiously.

"I like sweets," she said, "from people I know."

Mummy and Daddy froze a little.

"I know Sergeant Pritchard," she expanded it. "He is a good, kind policeman. He tells me the time. He finds me when I'm lost."

Sam Humphreys handed the sweets to his sergeant and Pritchard handed the bag to Zanny.

"Thank you," Zanny said, taking one. "You are most kind."

"And you," said Humphreys, "are a carefully brought up little girl. Mrs. Moncrief, I congratulate you."

Clare smiled wanly. She wondered if she should explain that it wasn't a deliberate snub and then decided that the smile was enough.

Graham said, "The gentleman who offered you a sweet, Zanny, is Detective Inspector Humphreys. He is a good man. A good, kind policeman."

"Not a bad man in a field who wants to take yer knickers orf," said Dolly thickly through her toffee.

Clare blushed.

Zanny noticed and was deeply indignant. "Knickers is rude."

"S'ruder without." Dolly who had arrived knickerless from Birmingham spoke with feeling.

Zanny felt a nibble of fear in her stomach. She wondered if the sweet were poisoned and then decided it wasn't. Retribution was by the rope and the knife. In any case, Dolly was eating her sweets with impunity.

All four adults, in an effort to channel the conversation back into sanity, spoke together and then stopped.

"We are here," Detective Inspector Humphreys said in his lay-preacher tone, "to find out how the little Morton child came to die. There will, of course, be an inquest, but it is necessary to know of the events leading up to his death." As well as taking the occasional service on a Sunday when there was a dearth of local preachers, Sam also took a Sunday School class. His role for this was different. He assumed it now.

"There is nothing nicer," he said, "than the innocent play of little children. What were you playing with Willie, Susannah, just before he died?"

Zanny was silent, in deep thought. What was a good game to play? What was a safe, nice game to play? In the reception class which Willie attended there was a game about buns in a baker's shop. Six little boy buns were bought by six little girl shoppers. It was a nice way of learning to count. Did it have to be a game?

"You were playing tag," Daddy said firmly. "You and Willie were having a game of tag. You were standing near the pool and Willie came charging at you. You ran away from him and he fell in. You told me. Don't you remember?"

"No," said Zanny.

"Then you told me," said Mummy.

"You didn't tell me," said Dolly.

"Tag is rough," Zanny said. "I don't play rough games."

23

A gentle game was pushing Monkey in her lovely doll's pram. The pram that Dolly might soon acquire. She looked at her contemplatively whilst awaiting inspiration.

"You was sittin' on the grass, all quiet like, teachin' 'im to read," Dolly said. "And I was sittin' in the buddly bush watchin' yer."

"Buddleia – the butterfly bush," Zanny corrected her, but without any show of superiority. Dolly despite her many faults was a quick thinker.

The older policeman looked at Dolly with a sharpening of interest. He hadn't been told she was in the vicinity. "So you saw what happened, Dolly?"

"In between readin' me book."

In the few months Dolly had been in Wales she had learnt to read remarkably quickly.

"About Winnie the Pooh," she added, guessing at the Inspector's scepticism. "It's a silly book," she added. Most middle-class books were.

"It isn't," Zanny dismissed the criticism with the contempt it deserved.

"It is. So's the Alice one. Fancy fallin' down a rabbit 'ole."

"People fall," Zanny pointed out. "Willie fell." It was a defence of literature, not a neat return to the subject matter.

The inspector addressed her again. "You like books, Susannah?"

"Sometimes." (Was it wrong to like books?)

"And you were teaching Willie to read?"

"Yes." (Words with an "h" – like hang?)

"You were sitting on the grass on a warm summer's day teaching him to read?"

"Yes."

"What made him get up and run into the pool?"

Zanny considered it. "He didn't like learning to read."

"So you played tag instead," Daddy interposed desperately.

24

"Please!" The Sunday School teacher and the lay-preacher became the Detective Inspector. "You must let the child tell it in her own way." He smiled falsely at Zanny. "Now – Susannah – let's go through it again. You were teaching Willie to read. He didn't like learning to read. Did you get cross with him?"

"Oh, no! I loved little Willie." Daddy's words came back to her. "Like a brother."

"Brothers get 'it." Dolly remembered her "h", "I used ter *h*it 'im. Zanny didn't *h*it 'im." She added, "She didn't 'it 'im when 'e stuffed the prickles down the back of 'er dress. She didn't chase 'im round the pool and she didn't push 'im in – she was all gentle like. She didn't sit on 'is 'ead neither – and there weren't no bubbles – nor no fish in 'is ear 'ole. If there 'ad been a fish in 'is ear 'ole, she'd 'ave squashed it with 'er sandal. She wouldn't let no fish nibble Willie – any more than she drownded 'im."

It was the longest speech Dolly had ever made in her life and she was well pleased with her performance. The pram was a beautiful shade of strawberry. She wondered if Zanny would throw in the embroidered pillow. The two little girls smiled at each other with a depth of complicity bordering on affection.

Zanny was the first to become aware of the arctic atmosphere. Mummy was like a statue of salt like the woman in the funny Bible story. Daddy looked as if he would happily decapitate Dolly and put her head on a spike. Sergeant Pritchard's eyes looked less amused. The old policeman looked positively malevolent.

"Zanny," he said, using her pet name with deceptive gentleness, "did you chase little Willie into the pond and drown him?"

"Oh, no!" Zanny said, "No – no – no!" She wasn't answering the question, but the inspector wasn't to know that. She was repudiating death – her own – messily and horribly contrived. And then, like the sun breaking through terrible storm clouds, she remembered and began to weep with relief.

25

"They've taken them away," she gasped. "They've taken the railings away. They sawed them off and put them on a lorry and took them to a factory to make aeroplanes for brave strong airmen like Daddy to fly over Germany because there's a nasty horrid war and people get killed – millions of people get killed all the time."

She got up and ran over to Daddy and flung herself onto his knee. He wouldn't let anything happen to her. The head bit was all right, but there was still her stomach and her neck. If they put her in a box like little Willie, then they would put all of her – head and all.

Daddy cuddled her. "It's all right, baby. Of course you didn't harm Willie. We all know that."

Her denial had been quite splendid. Histrionically superb. To cap it, Clare had begun to weep gently, too.

Good.

Splendid.

What was all that about railings? Not that it mattered.

Graham looked at Humphreys and then at Pritchard and knew the battle was won. His uniform added drama to the scene. He had been wise to wear it. Keep all this in perspective, Zanny's brilliant outburst had implied. We're fighting a war, gentlemen. One little evacuee has an accident. Tough. But I'm sweet – innocent – and six years old.

He took out his handkerchief and began mopping Zanny's eyes. Dolly looked on imperturbably.

The two policemen got up to go.

"I'm extremely sorry if we've distressed the little girl," Humphreys said. And even more sorry, he thought, that we've distressed her mother.

"Not at all," Graham said frostily.

"Will you be speaking to her again?" Clare asked through her silken wisp of a handkerchief.

Humphreys said that he wouldn't. He decided to

accept Moncrief's statement. The child was totally confused. Fancy being upset about the removal of railings now. Had she been guilty she wouldn't have thought of anything other than the crime. Crime? Guilty? A six-year-old? It really was a lot of nonsense. A wild little evacuee – a game of tag. That was it. Of course. What else?

He reached into his pocket for the bag of sweets again and pushed them into Zanny's hand. "There," he said, "there, there, it's all right."

Is it? Zanny thought, surprised. Is it really? It doesn't matter about Willie? You know about it and you don't care?

Luckily she kept the thought to herself. She snuffled and wept into Daddy's lovely blue uniform shoulder while Mummy showed the dear, kind – forgiving – policemen out.

Grandma Morton arrived on the afternoon train. Life had battered her for a long time and toughened her. Neither tender of soul nor of flesh she knew how to survive. The Lord, she believed, gave – but not very much – and what He gave He took away. She pictured Willie in the bosom of the Lord together with three of her other grandchildren and accepted it. She had long since ceased to question anything – except perhaps the goldfish pond. In the middle of a war it was wrong to have a goldfish pond. You couldn't eat goldfish. You had to *feed* goldfish. She stood glumly contemplating the pond while Clare and Graham stood unhappily beside her. The euphoria following the departure of the local police had given way to an honest though wary sympathy. Here was a blood relative. Here was someone who truly cared.

"We are most awfully sorry," Clare said for the second or third time. "We really are most awfully sorry."

"A most appalling accident," Graham said.

Grandma Morton, like a great many aged deaf, held

conversations in her mind which sometimes fell softly off her tongue like the susurration of dry leaves.

Clare, straining to hear, thought it might be a mumbled prayer – though surely the words fish and food had occurred? She didn't know what to say so she said "Amen".

Grandma Morton, embarrassed that her whisperings had left the locked parlour of her mind and reached the outside world, tried to cover up with a booming "Awful war, innit it?" It was her favourite catch-phrase and useful on all occasions – particularly this one. But for the awful war little Willie would still be living in Birmingham with his mum and dad. The death of his mum and dad was a much greater tragedy than the death of little Willie. When you were seventy-three you needed your son and his wife to cushion your few remaining years. You mourned little Willie, but he had been that much extra weight on your back. She had spent sleepless nights wondering what would happen to him and to little Dolly when she eventually passed on. This particular solution had been furthest from her mind – in fact, quite a shock.

She looked up at the sky. "Gawd moves in most mysterious ways," she said, "'is wonders to perform."

Clare, immensely relieved that the blame was to be attributed to celestial sources, smiled wanly at Graham. Relaxing perceptibly he smiled sadly back. It was lucky the old girl was so deaf. Whatever Zanny – or Dolly – might say would just bounce around harmlessly. Well, he hoped it would. Reparation of some kind would have to be made to the old woman. Keeping Dolly with them and doing the best they could for her was the only reparation he could think of. Despite its hazards, it had to be done. A present of cash, though obviously badly needed, would be so much blood money. A hamper of black market food wouldn't have any sinister implications. The farms around had plenty of butter and eggs and bacon. It wouldn't be difficult to drum up local sympathy. The old biddy would return to Birmingham laden with gifts.

In the meantime the inquest had to be got through this afternoon – and then the funeral.

Grandma Morton who had attended many funerals in her time had never attended an inquest. She sat through this one, dozing after a heavy lunch and not hearing a word of it, to be told by a radiant Clare at the end that it was accidental death, which, of course, she knew already. She wondered why Clare looked so pleased. The Squadron Leader looked pleased, too, but in a more restrained way. He was sorry he couldn't stay on the extra few days for the funeral, he told her, but he had to return to his air base. "Awful war, innit it?" she said, excusing him, and he agreed. In a moment of brilliant character assessment he slipped her a small bottle of gin to drink in bed if she found sleep elusive. "To drown me sorrows," she said, interpreting it her way.

Dolly, who had watched the surreptitious gift being passed, frowned in disapproval. Zanny's posh folks never got pissed – or if they did they got pissed politely. They didn't sit up in bed in the middle of the night and sing "Abide With Me" and then break the chamber pot by falling onto it in the dark. She listened, crimson-cheeked, as Clare took her grandmother to the bathroom to clean her up. Zanny, who had been awakened by the crash, went to see what was happening. The only grandmother she had ever had any contact with was Mummy's mummy who was known as Grandmamma. She wore a white hair-piece to camouflage her thinning hair and at night put her teeth in a glass bowl with a lid on it. She used Pears transparent soap and cleaned her skin nightly with Oatine cream. Her nightdress was woolly and white with lace at the neck and wrists and her feet were clean. She smelled nice.

Grandma Morton was different.

Zanny, unobserved by Mummy who was too distraught

to notice (why the *hell* had Graham behaved like a lunatic?), made a note of all the differences and then went into Dolly's bedroom to report on them.

She sat on the end of the bed in the dark and wrapped the eiderdown around her.

"My grandmamma," she said, "doesn't need bathing."

Dolly was silent.

"And she doesn't do silly things in the night."

Dolly wriggled lower in the bed.

"When she sings hymns, she sings them in church. And she doesn't need sticking plaster on her bottom."

Dolly, despite her shame, giggled. She hoped very much that Grandma would return to Birmingham in double quick time after the funeral and not stay on here doing things she shouldn't. Zanny's mummy hadn't de-nitted her – and the bath tonight had been forced by circumstances – but she had put a rubber under the sheet when she thought no one was looking. Grandma, later, had taken it out and hidden it in the wardrobe.

"Wot does she think I am," she had asked Dolly, aggrieved, "inconnynent?"

"Mattresses don't grow on trees," Dolly had replied, mystifying her.

Dolly's blood bond might be with Grandma, but blood tended to run thin when not satisfactorily nourished. Her bond with Clare was the bond of a comfortable environment. There were rats in the Birmingham tenement, here there was a dear little hamster. Bread and marge and dripping didn't compare with Clare's well-stocked larder. In Birmingham you were sometimes hungry, you were often cold. The Germans dropped bombs on you. Here your little brother got drowned in a goldfish pool, but you were warm and well fed and your nightie had yellow roses on it. A golden-haired little murderess sat on your feet at the bottom of the bed, but the bed was in a pretty room in a lovely house with a beautiful garden ... with a pool in it. She could cope with the pool. She could cope with Zanny. Today Zanny

30

had given her the strawberry-coloured doll's pram. As arranged.

"Will you go back with your Grandma?" Zanny, zooming in on her thoughts, asked hopefully.

"Will I *heck*!" Dolly retorted, breathing out the aspirate explosively. "And get off me bleedin' feet."

It would be unwise, Clare decided, in fact it would be too harrowing, for Zanny to attend the funeral. She wasn't at all sure that Dolly should go either, but couldn't do anything about it when Grandma Morton insisted. The service wouldn't put thumb-screws on Dolly's conscience. Her conscience was clear and sweet. Zanny's conscience was beyond Clare's understanding. When you were that young you probably didn't even have one. Her own Catholic childhood came back to her. She had gone to her first confession at the age of seven – at the age of seven you were supposed to know. Zanny, at six, quite obviously didn't. And with some considerable luck no one else would know either.

It was a very moving service. Everyone, including Clare, wept.

Zanny, who had spent the afternoon in the care of a neighbour, returned in time for the funeral tea at four. The tea was laid on the dining-room table. There were plates of ham and salad and little glass dishes of fresh fruit salad and cream. Mummy served her coldly, almost with dislike, and Zanny felt goosepimples on her arms and legs. The only person who took much notice of her and was kind was the Reverend Daniel Edwards of the Baptist chapel. He sat her on his knee and peeled her an apple and taught her how to count in Welsh. His breath smelled of tobacco and his knees were like the bony carcases of dead fowl but when you suddenly found yourself in the wilderness you embraced any Man Friday who happened along. She ate the apple delicately, her head a little averted, and assumed an attitude of

31

enjoyment. "You are a nice little girl," he told her, "a very nice little girl." Mummy, overhearing, wasn't impressed. It had been a very small coffin – a very deep hole. Perhaps Zanny should have gone after all. Perhaps she should have been frog-marched there and made to look.

On the day after the funeral Clare began to worry that Grandma Morton might want to stay on. Reparation for the horrendous sins of one's offspring didn't quite stretch to an indefinite putting up with a protracted visit. On that score, however, she needn't have worried. Grandma Morton's values were somewhat different from Dolly's. The air of gentility here was so rarefied that it hurt her lungs to breathe. Crisp white bed linen dared one to defile it. The comfortable, sheetless bed at home, humped up with ancient blankets, had the sleep-inducing embrace of a disreputable kindly old friend. Here the food was good and plentiful but if so much as a morsel got stuck in the cavity of your last remaining tooth it had to lie there in painful politeness. At home you stuck your finger in and gouged it out. It was comfortable to be mannerless and dirty and to sing inebriated hymns to a God who sat up there somewhere above the German aeroplanes and willed the bombs to their appointed destinations. That life was mapped out in advance was something Grandma Morton implicitly believed. Her own life, she was sure, would continue in a Birmingham tenement amongst friends who went with her to the air-raid shelter and helped out with the rations when the need arose. Those that hadn't got anything very much were on the whole liberal with it. It was a tolerant community, rough-edged but aware. That Dolly should so obviously be happy to rise out of it and into this surprised her. She had come prepared to take her home if she wanted to come, and was relieved that she didn't. The parting would be permanent at some stage in the future and God no doubt knew what He was doing by planning for her to stay. Mrs. Moncrief wasn't the picture of an ideal mother figure, but Nancy, Dolly's mum, hadn't been either. It was a pity Mrs. Moncrief wasn't the same shape and size as Nancy. The winter coat she had offered hadn't fitted and her shoes were daft. As a final polite gesture she decided she would wear them to the station and put on her plimsolls when the train was on its way. They were good, floggable leather and should fetch something at uncle's.

The station was a little over a quarter of a mile away down a winding road thickly hedged with briar and honeysuckle. The mountains, sombre as calvinist chapels, brooded greyly in the warm sun. Dolly, proud possessor of the strawberry pram, pushed it happily. It contained a carpet bag full of dairy produce including eggs wrapped carefully in an angora jumper. Her grandmother and Zanny's mum walked behind slowly – speed, or the lack of it, being dictated by the pressure on Grandma's bunions. Zanny, hotly resentful that the pram was no longer hers, masked it by singing vicious little ditties about cock robin and pussy down the well. "Who saw him die?" she trilled, "I said the fly, with my little eye." Catching Mummy's expression she skipped ahead and began gathering flowers. "Ding – dong – bell – pussy down the well," she warbled. "Who pushed him in? Little Tommy thin . . ."

Grandma Morton hearing tunes, not words, couldn't make out why Mrs. Moncrief was scowling. Perhaps she was afraid that the eggs would break in the angora jumper and spoil it. Perhaps she thought her own daughter should be pushing the pram. Dolly had said that the pram was hers now – a present. If she believed that, then her brain was beginning to soften. That was the worst of living in a place like this – you began seeing the world out there like something in the talkies. No longer real. You stopped taking much notice of it. You sat in your plush cinema seat and were warm and cosy. Eventually you went to sleep.

She began thinking of all the films she had seen.

33

Zanny looked like Shirley Temple. Dolly, despite being clean, could have come straight out of "Our Gang". She had her hair washed once a week, and a bath every night, and still she wanted to stay. Well, good luck to her.

She whispered and muttered and wheezed and cursed her shoes and boomed out occasionally about the war and about being all sweaty and hoping she wouldn't lose the train. Clare, echoing the hope, sprinted on ahead when she saw it waiting in the station. One of the advantages of living in a village was the power to hold back a train long enough to get an old woman aboard it. With the aid of the porter who doubled as station master, Mrs. Morton was pushed up into a carriage and her luggage bundled in after her.

"Kiss your Grandma," Clare ordered Dolly, but neither Dolly nor Grandma took any notice.

"Skelp 'er if she don't be'ave," Grandma said fondly, easing off her shoes. It was good to be going home to dirty, smelly Birmingham. Here even the station was clean. The steam from the engine wisped up into the blue sky like soap suds. "And don't forget ter clean yer teeth, Dolly," she added, humour tinged with bitterness. Ivory castles they called them in this neck of the woods, how ruddy stupid could you get? She felt more cut off from Dolly now than she did from Willie. He, at least, had departed to God's bosom as she had remembered him – runny nose and all.

She leaned out of the window and ran her hand roughly through Dolly's hair and noticed that Zanny stepped smartly back in case she did the same to hers. Funny kid – that one. Her mum should stop stuffing her with codliver oil and malt. She stuffed Dolly with it, too, but it made no difference. Bean thin – Dolly. Always would be.

Her parting words were to Clare as the train began to steam off. "Goldfish," she said, "aint right. Yer rubber's in the wardrobe. God bless."

34

Clare, unable to contribute a rational reply, waved mutely as the train steamed off into the distance.

The gloom that had settled on her spirits since the death of Willie began to rise a little. Everything had gone off very well. In time she might be able to train her mind to believe that it really had been an accident. Even if it hadn't been, the act had been impulsive, not planned. Her dislike of Zanny after the funeral had been a shameful reaction. Zanny was a little child. For most of the time she was a good little child. Had she been a quarrelsome, nasty, vicious child she would be making a fuss about the pram that Dolly was pushing. She had let her push it all the way to the station and now she was letting her push it all the way back. Perhaps she was sorry for what she had done. Of course she was sorry. Her loan of the pram to Dolly was her way of showing it.

She held her hand out to Zanny in a conciliatory gesture. "Hold hands with Mummy, darling – while Dolly has your pram?"

Zanny declined politely. She began singing again, a slow, muttered little dirge. "Three blind mice . . . see how they run . . ." She ran ahead of Dolly and up the brow of the hill. "Cut off their heads with a carving knife." She stopped. "Cut off their *tails* with a carving knife." Heads was better. Heads could not be stuck on railings when there were no railings there. In the distance she could see the green van of Evans the Bread winding down the road towards them. He was a nice man – Evans the Bread. He had given her an extra hot-cross bun last Easter. He had given one to Dolly, too. He shouldn't have given one to Dolly. Dolly didn't belong here. She came and took things.

She began running back down the hill to Dolly and the strawberry pram. "Did you ever hear such a thing in your life," she bellowed, "as three blind mice?"

Dolly's hard little hands were clutching the pram handle as Zanny came up to her. Dolly, wary as a forest

35

creature, felt the adrenalin flow, and the small hairs at the nape of her neck tingled as she prepared herself. The van was around the corner now, big and lumbering and coming at some speed. Zanny, with beautiful timing, hurled herself at Dolly, but Dolly, with even better timing, pivoted on her heels, tried to keep hold of the pram, failed and let it go. Evans the Bread saw with horror a child about to be killed – swerved into a pink object that shattered into the bonnet – and then the van careered out of control and smashed through the low wall and into an ancient oak tree.. The petrol tank exploded and flames leapt twenty feet into the branches.

Zanny smelt burnt bread – or it might have been burnt Evans the Bread. She could see him still sitting in the driver's seat, half way up the tree. He was black like Guy Fawkes on a bonfire. And then she looked for her pram and couldn't recognise it. Dolly was perfectly recognisable. She was sitting in the ditch, glaring. "You've smashed me bleedin' pram," she wailed. "Watcher gone and done that for – yer silly cow?" And then she turned and looked up at the blazing tree. "Cor!" she said.

Clare, silent until that moment, began to have hysterics. Laughter slashed her with knives and the tears poured down her cheeks. She went down on her knees in the grass verge and buried her face in a clump of bracken. She laughed and she howled. When she eventually sat up she saw Zanny looking down at her.

"I didn't mean to kill him," Zanny said. "And I didn't mean to break the pram." Her lips trembled.

"No," Mummy said, very coldly, very calmly, "I know."

Two

The Convent, two centuries old, and built of mellow stone, was beautifully sited south of the Lleyn Peninsula. It was a very select boarding school for girls run by a teaching order of nuns. The syllabus stressed the fact that each child had individual attention and the number of pupils rarely rose above fifty. Emphasis was laid on character building. The spiritual and academic sides of the pupils were carefully nurtured so that the finished product, the syllabus implied, would be a young lady of considerable refinement. She would be good in every sense of the word. She might even one day be a nun – though no pressure would be brought to bear.

"Both the children are, of course, Catholics?" Mother Benedicta enquired.

Clare, a lapsed Catholic, had been prepared for the question and had decided that for a while at least she would re-enter the fold. Graham, nominally Church of England, didn't give a damn one way or the other. While Zanny had been busy murdering the breadman he had been busy dropping bombs on Cologne. His own activity he could forgive, but beloved child as she was, he couldn't quite bring himself to forgive Zanny. He was quite willing to put her anywhere – even in a Zen monastery – if it would do any good. Quite obviously Clare couldn't cope – perhaps these nuns here could. Mother Benedicta, whom he regarded as the chief religious female, seemed sufficiently formidable. It was a French order and she was called Ma Mère though she was in fact Irish. Most of the nuns were Irish. He wished she would offer him a drink of her native Guinness – or better still some scotch. The last few weeks had been hell – and he wasn't thinking of the war. You got used to that.

"My husband and I," Clare said, "are happy that both children should be instructed in the Catholic faith."

It was an adroit side-stepping and Mother Benedicta recognised it as such. "I can accept your religious plans for Susannah," she said, "but the other child, you tell me, is an evacuee. I think her parents should have some say in the matter."

"She's a war orphan," Clare explained. "We can't even trace her grandmother now."

This was true. Grandma Morton might have regarded it as the mysterious working of the Lord to arrange for a bomb to demolish most of the street where she lived very shortly after Zanny's own piece of demolition work. Graham, whose compassionate leave seemed to be spent in crisis situations, had spent some while trying to get news of her, but had drawn a blank. The fact that he would soon be drafted abroad, possibly to North Africa, he was beginning to regard with some relief. Let Clare bed her doctor friend. Let Zanny deplete the population in her own inimitable way. Let him fly his bombers in peace.

"But," Mother Benedicta pointed out, "you are not Dorothy Morton's official guardians."

Dorothy Morton, Clare thought, you have not yet met. Neither have I. Neither has anybody. She is Dolly and she still wipes her nose on her sleeve.

"If you will have her," she said, "we are quite prepared to pay her fees – buy all her clothes – be responsible for her until she is old enough to look after herself. If we have to become her official guardians to do all that – then we will – won't we?" This to Graham.

He agreed. All this had been decided before they came. Clare, Graham was beginning to realise, was maturing with the speed of a tropical plant in a rain forest. The pretty, daisy-like little woman of a few weeks ago was becoming positively orchidaceous. She was pink-

38

cheeked, dominating, to be reckoned with. Most of this was due to desperation. Dolly couldn't be ditched. Zanny couldn't be incarcerated in solitary confinement. The convent as a compromise was the only possible solution. The convent was neutral ground. Here there was no Monkey. No pink pram. It was unlikely that Zanny would covet Dolly's rosary beads. If she did – then tough. Let Mother Benedicta remove the dagger. Her own mother had had enough.

"Both children," Mother Benedicta pointed out, "are very young. Six, you tell me, and seven?"

"Yes – but according to your prospectus you have children even younger."

"Only because their parents are unable for various reasons – mainly connected with the war – to have them with them. Your home is comparatively safe in a small village not so far from here. Unlike many of the parents you are not in an area of heavy bombing. You are robbing yourself of some of the joys of motherhood by sending them away so young."

Clare was careful not to look at Graham. "The joys of motherhood," she said, "I am prepared to forego."

"May I ask why?"

"Because it is better for both children that they should be here. I can't look after them as well as I should. I haven't the right type of temperament. I'm sure you and the other nuns have." (You even carry keys like a wardress and I've seen your nice neat little cells with a picture of the Bleeding Heart in them. You'll cope. Please God, the Blessed Virgin, and all the Holy Saints, you'll cope.)

Mother Benedicta's slightly bulbous eyes looked like twin flares on a runway guiding an off-course aeroplane home. She turned them on Graham. "Why," she demanded, "should your wife believe she hasn't the temperament to look after two young children? Or do you think she can manage perfectly well?"

When captured by the enemy you gave your name,

rank and number; you didn't impart unnecessary information. It was perfectly acceptable to invent. The truth, however, if it did no harm, was the best bet.

"Our daughter, Zanny," he said, "is jealous of Dolly. We can't handle it. We're sure you can."

Mother Benedicta stood up and went over to a bell by the fireplace and pushed it. In a few minutes Sister Bernadette would come in with a tray of tea for three. The problem here was quite obviously no problem at all. What child wasn't jealous of another child? The mother was particularly sensitive. She had no hesitation now about accepting the two little girls. They must be trained to love one another in the Lord. In the meantime there was the question of fees. The little evacuee would probably be extremely backward – extra tuition in reading might be in order. She began making an inventory of all the business details. Money was important, after all.

"As it's war-time," she said, "we have to do the best we can with the clothing coupons. The uniform used to be a dark blue dress with a white Peter Pan collar. Now, it's the rather ubiquitous gymslip. Still dark blue, I'm pleased to say, worn with a white blouse. The winter coat, once grey, is now navy-blue. Can you manage all this for the two of them?"

Clare, who would have raided Harrods if necessary, said she could.

They were in – that was all that mattered. The angelus began to toll. Ding-dong-bell, Clare thought. Board up the convent well. She reached over to Graham and touched his hand. He squeezed it.

It didn't seem fair to Dolly that she should be committed to a convent because Zanny had tried to kill her. On the whole, she thought, she would rather be dead. She had liked the little village school. She had liked its smell of chalk – of wild flowers on the window sills. There were flowers here, banks of them, around statues with naked feet or with sandals with strips between the toes. The flowers were real but they looked as waxen as the statues and they didn't smell. There was a funny pong in the church. It came out of a little gold thing on a chain which a boy swung when he followed the priest. She couldn't see the sense of being deliberately choked with the stuff. If Jesus wanted scent, why didn't He have Attar of Roses, or something? This stuff stank. She had made the suggestion to one of the nuns and the nun, shocked, had told her she'd pray for her. "Ta," Dolly had said bitterly, "ta, very much."

Zanny, on the whole, took to her new surroundings with an almost adult resignation. It was due to happen to her anyway in the course of time. All the Moncriefs had gone to boarding school. The Bradys on Mummy's side had gone to convents, which was much the same thing. It was right to go away to school when you were young; perhaps not this young, but young. The only difference in her case was that Mummy had got tired of her rather quicker than usual. Mummy's displeasure was like dowsing all the fires in the house – you shivered in the cold. That the fiery end of Evans the Bread might have something to do with it, Zanny was wise enough to guess. Not that anybody had made any fuss about that. The dear, kind policemen hadn't asked her anything. Here there was no atmosphere of censure. Here she was accepted. For one thing, she spoke like everyone else. She handled her knife and fork properly in the refectory. She didn't spit. And on the rare occasions when the air-raid siren sounded and everyone trooped down to the convent cellars, the older girls took it in turn to sit her on their knees. She was a golden-haired little pet, they said, an adorable little sweetie.

Dolly, sitting on the broad end of a P.E. balancing frame because all the chairs had been taken, saw all this and didn't care. Let them go soft over Zanny. If this were a zoo and not an air-raid shelter they'd ooh and aah over cuddly little bears and leopards and orang-

41

utans. If tarantula spiders didn't look like tarantula spiders they'd probably ooh and aah over them, too. This last thought was prompted by a large spider which was crawling up the wall behind Sister Philomena. She gazed at it, willing it to drop on to the stiff white bit of fancy headgear that the nuns wore to jazz up the black.

Sister Philomena, misinterpreting the reason for Dolly's screwed up expression, suggested gently that she might like to sit on her lap. The child was quite obviously frightened. She had probably had some terrifying experiences of bombing in Birmingham. Here, nobody was scared. There had, so far, been nothing to be scared about. The characteristic engine note of German bombers thrumming overhead was something you got used to. A few months ago one had offloaded its bombs during combat with a fighter. They had made rather a mess of a turnip field, but that was all.

Dolly declined the invitation.

"Dear child," Sister Philomena soothed, "you mustn't be afraid."

"It ain't that I particlry mind 'em," Dolly said, "it's just that I don't want 'em gettin' close. Me Grandma didn't mind 'em at all."

"Good, brave Grandma," said Sister Philomena, who had heard the news about Grandma – missing believed dead. "The good Lord blessed her with a courageous heart."

Brave enough, Dolly thought, to pick them up and stamp on them. That her courage to kill spiders was God-given surprised her. "I threw a brick at one once," she said, "and nearly got 'im."

A vision of a defiant child hurling a brick – probably in imagination – at an enemy bomber, filled Sister Philomena with warm affection. Here was a little outcast – an orphan – a child that the other children ignored – or laughed at. Here was a Cause – a Good Work – a Soul to be trimmed up and polished and made desirable and lovely. Here was a reason for being in this

42

convent in Wales – for being in a convent at all. Satan, of late, had been digging around for reasons. Here was a possible gem. Rough, no doubt, but what a challenge. Oh, what a challenge!

It dawned on the nuns slowly that once they got rid of their first impression of Dolly and began looking at her they were looking at someone rather exceptional. The infants teacher in the village school had known it, but she hadn't been asked to make a report on the child. Dolly's mind, like virgin soil, was rich in potential. Whatever was put in it flourished. True, her acceptance and rejection of certain seeds was highly selective. She could read most books with ease. That she should prefer a copy of *Dracula* which someone had smuggled into the library to any of the milder books on the shelves was characteristic. She read it in a couple of nights, under the bed-clothes, by the aid of a torch, and then repeated it as a serial to anyone who wanted to listen. In time, quite a lot wanted to listen. The outcast, who hadn't cared about being an outcast, had found her own way in.

The story sessions took place surreptitiously in one of the music cubicles. There were ten of these with a piano in each. They were sound-proofed. In the open space in the centre of the room a naïve young novice sat at a desk and looked at all the pianos being thumped away behind glass, and at the little group in the last cubicle who were sitting on the floor having a theory quiz. When she occasionally opened the door to see how they were getting on with it she was greeted with a chorus about crotchets and quavers and demi-semi-quavers. One or two, she noticed, seemed to be pale with terror, but perhaps her glasses needed changing. Not an easy subject, music theory; you needed a mathematical mind for it.

Zanny never attended these sessions. In Dolly's parlance, she considered them daft. That Dolly should have acolytes annoyed her a little, but within safe emotional boundaries. This was, indeed, neutral ground and she had friends of her own. Plenty of them. But she hadn't a nun. Dolly had Sister Philomena. She might have felt rather better about this had she known about Dolly's feelings on the matter. Dolly would, with great pleasure, have presented Zanny with Sister Philomena, who decidedly wasn't Monkey or a pink pram. Sister Philomena was a flaming nuisance. That she was a flaming nuisance – with the "g" carefully sounded – and not a bleedin' pain in the arse, was due to Sister Philomena's elocution lessons. They went on for an hour every Wednesday evening between six and seven, which was after prep time and before supper time and was officially play time. Dolly grudged the period very bitterly.

The lessons took place in the parlour which was used for receiving guests. The chairs were of red plush with white antimacassars on them. There was an oval table in the centre, highly polished, with a circular white embroidered cloth in the middle of it. In the middle of the cloth was a brass flower pot filled with maidenhair fern. On Dolly's first visit a rose lay beside the pot. Sister Philomena told Dolly to pick it up.

Dolly, scrutinising it suspiciously for thorns, did so.

"That," said Sister Philomena, her eyes shining with the self-deluding euphoria of those who think they are being truly good, "is you, Dolly."

Dolly had rubbed shoulders in the past with the drunk and the insane (sozzled, funny in the 'ead) but she hadn't met this kind of aberration before and didn't know how to place it, so she said nothing.

"Has it ever occurred to you," Sister Philomena went on, "that you are beautiful – as that rose is beautiful – a creature of God – delicately fashioned – created with love?"

"I know what me mum and dad did, if that's what you mean," Dolly said. When you lived in one room you couldn't help but know. The end product in every case was a screaming baby – not a red rose with a greenfly on

44

it. She picked the greenfly off and flipped it onto the carpet. Didn't these nuns know *anything*? Was that why they were here?

"Don't you know nothink?" she asked.

Sister Philomena felt herself blush. The task was going to be more formidable than she had expected. She rushed on quickly before Dolly could start lecturing her on copulation.

"Out there," she said, waving her hand in the direction of the convent gardens, "you can hear the birds sing. They sing very beautifully. God has given them a voice box and they know how to use it. You, too, have a voice box. You, too, can produce beautiful sounds."

"Ain't got no ear for it," Dolly said. During the school play at the village school she had been told to mime the words of "While Shepherds Watched" and not to dare let a squeak out. Miss Williams had been down to earth, very sensible. She had earned Dolly's respect.

"Those that have ears," Sister Philomena said, "let them hear. You have ears, Dolly, two pretty little pink ones like shells on a beach. They are wonderful ears – as good as anyone else's ears. They will listen to sounds and then you will reproduce them. Take the sound *ing*, for instance. Ting-a-ling – a-*ling*. Can you say that after me? Ting-a-*ling* – a-*ling*. Emphasis on the *ing*."

"Oh, Gawd!" said Dolly quietly.

What couldn't be escaped had to be endured; she had learnt this from her grandmother. Sister Philomena's zeal was as strong as any of the impositions she had been forced to put up with in the past. The hour, she found out eventually, became an hour-and-a-half if you failed to comply. You escaped quicker if you sounded your h's and your g's. When you saw a double negative coming up you skirted it carefully or you were stuck with the ruddy thing for another ten minutes. If you were told to look like a rose – speak like a nightingale – and walk like a princess – you were careful not to fart in exasperation, (the penalty for that had been an extra hour slotted in on the following evening). One learned to compromise.

Towards the end of the term Dolly had lowered the flag of rebellion sufficiently, on the surface at least, to become socially acceptable. She was beginning to sound right. She was on the first rung of the class ladder. She now picked her nose in private. Her finger-nails were clean because there was a daily nail inspection and you had to go back and clean them if they weren't. There wasn't an ear inspection, but she had become obsessional about ears, which wasn't surprising. They were the only part of her anatomy that she cleaned of her own free will.

Zanny, not interested in the metamorphosis of Dolly from a grub into a rather sticky creature with embryo wings, was busy finding her own level. Academically it was a couple of classes below Dolly. In the past she had been able to correct Dolly's pronunciation and been pleased to do so. Now, Dolly was mistress of the hard words. To lose one's feeling of superiority was like losing one's vest – somewhat chilly. For the most part Clare's plan of separation was working out, the two children saw little of each other – mainly from choice. Preparation for their first communion altered matters.

Mother Benedicta wrote to Clare reminding her that as it was soon to be Zanny's seventh birthday arrangements were about to be made for her first communion preceded by her first confession. Dolly, too, was going to be accepted into the Church. Perhaps Mrs. Moncrief would like to send white dresses for both of them? The convent would provide the white veils. As regards a cake, ingredients these days were rather difficult to come by. Perhaps Mrs. Moncrief had foreseen this and put a quantity of sugar aside?

Clare, a little lulled that so far the population of the convent hadn't diminished, had been living in a fairly cosy present. Graham, as expected, had been posted to North Africa and wrote as often as he could. He sent kisses to Zanny which Clare passed on. On the surface they were still very loving parents of a dear little daughter. That the dear daughter was soon to be embraced by Mother Church after confessing all her sins was a bit of a jolt. Clare didn't know what to do. Writing to Graham wouldn't alter events. A worry shared wasn't, in this case, a worry halved. She didn't dare tell Peter. He still made her back better, as Zanny put it. They were both accomplished lovers and neither thought beyond the act. The complication of love – of family commitment, of the future – had no part in the relationship.

Zanny's future in the shape of a confessional loomed on Clare's horizon like a cross of doom. How sealed would the priest's lips be? If not sealed, would she be thrown out? After several sleepless nights Clare decided to await events and not anticipate them. There was nothing she could do, short of visiting Zanny and telling her to keep her mouth shut and as, no doubt, she was being trained right now to do the opposite there didn't seem any point in wasting her breath. She wasn't any good at sewing, but she had kept her white wedding dress and decided to let the local dressmaker make a couple of communion dresses out of it. The cake she made herself. The marzipan was fake, but the rest of the ingredients weren't too difficult to come by. One of the farmers' wives even managed to rustle up some dried fruit. Good strong Welsh non-conformists, they might be, with an inborn distrust of Papist practices, but when it came to providing a cake for two little girls, one of whom had lost her dear little brother so tragically, they were prepared to help all they could.

Meanwhile neither Zanny nor Dolly could under- stand what all the fuss was about. Dolly absorbed the catechism like a sponge. The quicker you learnt things, the quicker you were let off the hook. Zanny, whose memory wasn't nearly as good, found that by smiling sweetly at Father Donovan she achieved similar

47

results. The old priest was delighted with them. Dear little daughters of God. One so clever and quick. One so pretty and good.

Two little queens, the nuns cooed over them as they stood in their white dresses, clutching their white missals, with their white veils draped over their hair.

Clare, in the congregation for the Big Event, saw them entering the church and felt a hard thump of apprehension followed by an unexpected desire to weep. Zanny looked so *pretty*. She looked *angelic*. Why couldn't she be as she looked? Dolly, in contrast, looked bizarre. Funny little monkey face. Huge dark eyes. The dress was half an inch too long and she kept tripping over it. Someone had given her a large handkerchief edged with lace and it was sticking out of her left sleeve.

Dolly was the first to go into the confessional. Who she was pleasing by going through all this ritual she wasn't sure. If Grandma hadn't escaped the bomb and was flying around up there her eyes would be popping out of her head.

The quicker it was said, the quicker it was finished.

"Bless me, Father, for I have sinned."

Father Donovan, on the other side of the partition, rolled out his response. "May the Lord be in thy heart and on thy lips that thou mayest truly and humbly confess thy sins, in the name of the Father and of the Son and of the Holy Ghost."

"Amen," said Dolly.

The priest prompted her gently, "And what do you wish to confess?"

Dolly thought about it. She had thought about it a great deal. She had watched the nuns kneeling before going into confession. They undid their veils so that they drooped over their faces. What, she wondered, did they confess? What crime could be committed in a place like this? They must be daft.

"Nothing," she said.

"Nothing? Think – child – think."

"I ain't done nothing." In times of stress – and this was becoming a time of stress – Dolly reverted to her natural tongue.

Father Donovan, remembering how bright she had been at the catechism classes, was a little taken aback. He had never heard her speak like that before. "If you haven't done anything," he said, "you might have committed a sin of omission. By not doing anything in a particular situation you might have sinned."

Dolly had a vague memory of a similar, though simpler, conversation held with him – something about it being right to help a blind person across a road, and being a sin if you didn't. Here, there weren't any blind people, and you didn't get out all that often to cross roads.

She waited for some more suggestions.

He came out with several – including spiritual pride – and Dolly hotly denied all of them. She didn't even know what spiritual pride meant.

They were both beginning to sweat.

She wanted to get out. She'd had enough. She couldn't see his face, but his voice sounded cross. If she couldn't come up with a sin soon he'd come out from his side and thump her.

And then she remembered and began to grin with relief. Of course she'd sinned. She'd told him a whopping big lie as soon a she'd entered the box. "Bless me, Father, for I have sinned," she'd said. She'd told him she'd sinned when she hadn't.

"Father, I sinned by telling a lie."

"Well, thank God for that," Father Donovan said acidly. "And thank the Blessed Virgin for helping you to remember."

He decided not to ask what the lie was, she had already been with him ten minutes and it was time to get on to the other little lass, who might prove more fruitful. He curtly told her to say three Hail Marys.

Zanny, waiting for Dolly to come out, was getting

more and more nervous. What was she telling him that took all this time to tell?

At last Dolly, showing obvious signs of strain, emerged. In her haste to leave the confessional she tripped over her dress and sprawled full length in front of Zanny. "Bleedin' 'eck!" she muttered, embarrassed. And then whispered to Zanny that she had been given three Hail Marys.

While Zanny was settling herself in the confessional Father Donovan sent up a brief prayer that this one would be easier. They went through the preliminaries and then got down to business.

"It is sometimes a little difficult to bring sins to mind, but you've had a little time to think, child. Now what have you got to confess?"

There was silence for a moment or two – a little rustling of the satin dress – and then a conspiratorial little whisper.

"Father, can you hear me if I don't say it loud?"

"I can hear you perfectly, child."

"I drowned little Willie."

"What?"

"I drowned little Willie – in the goldfish pond."

Father Donovan put his index finger in his ear and explored for anything that might be blocking it.

"Did you say dragged?"

"No – drowned. I sat on his head."

Dear God Almighty, Father Donovan thought, what kind of game are You playing with me this day? He had always credited the Blessed Lord with a sense of humour, but he had never been teased by Him before. First one child hasn't sinned at all – and then finally obliges after much coaxing. The other child invents a whopping marvellous one. Straight off.

"It is wrong," he said severely, "to tell a lie."

"Oh, I know, Father. And it's wrong not to tell the truth, isn't it?"

A little niggle of doubt entered Father Donovan's

mind. She sounded so very sure of herself. Very grave. Not a ripple of laughter. It wasn't beyond the bounds of possibility.

"How old," he asked, "was little – er – Willie?"

"Four."

Perfectly, appallingly, possible.

He dropped the pretence of not knowing who was on the other side of the partition. "Zanny?"

"Yes, Father."

"Are you telling me the truth, Zanny?"

"Yes, Father."

"Dear Christ! Why in the name of God did he let you?"

"Let me what, Father?"

"Sit on his head."

"I chased him into the pond – he fell and banged his head on the bottom – before he could get up I sat on his head – he tried to push me off, but he couldn't. There was bubbles all over the place – and fish. When Mummy and the doctor got him out he was dead."

A graphic, very clear, explanation. Father Donovan believed it. He rested his head in his hands and had a sudden very strong desire to go to the lavatory, which he resisted. He had heard a whole range of sins in his time – one or two quite hairy ones – but none as hairy as this. He didn't know what to say – or do.

"Father."

He groaned. "Yes, Zanny?"

"Do I tell all my sins at once – or spread them out?"

"You mean – there's something else?"

"Yes, Father. I murdered Evans the Bread."

"Who?"

"Mr. Evans who drives the breadvan. I exploded him. He sat halfway up a tree – all black – with flames coming out of him. He died."

"Oh," said Father Donovan. His bowels settled back into normality. The Blessed Lord was having a field day of it, today. He had almost got him believing it. What was his own sin? Being pompous? He had accused the

51

other child of spiritual pride and now the Lord was pulling his leg like crazy. He had sent him this child – with her terrible imagination – and for half a minute there he had believed what she was telling him. He saw suddenly that she was an instrument of the Lord, this golden-haired creature, sent to him with the gift of laughter – of laughter at himself. Her only sin was reading the wrong sort of comics and then identifying with them. The nuns shouldn't allow that sort of literature into the building. Evans the Bread – that was a new one!

His voice shook with laughter which he did his best to suppress. "You know, Zanny, that it's wrong to tell a lie?"

"Yes, Father."

"Very wrong."

"Yes, Father."

"And you won't tell any more lies, will you, Zanny?"

"No, Father." (How could you tell more when you hadn't told any?)

"Zanny."

"Yes, Father."

"You know it's wrong to read the wrong sort of books. What sort of books do you read?"

"Peter Pan," Zanny suggested cautiously. Taking grasshopper leaps after his mind was tiring her.

"What about comics?"

"*Chick's Own* and *Rainbow*."

"Have you ever read any nasty comics belonging to boys?"

"No, Father."

"About people like Evans the Bread – or was it Evans the Dread?"

"No, Father."

"And if no is a lie you won't do it any more, will you, Zanny?"

Zanny, totally confused, said she wouldn't.

"Then say three Hail Marys, child, and bless you."

52

"Is that all?" Zanny in her most pessimistic moments had imagined herself being drowned in holy water or burnt at the stake.

"Yes," Father Donovan said cheerfully, "that's all, unless you'd like to say a little prayer for me."

It was when she was in bed that night that Zanny began taking apart the puzzle and putting it together again in a way that made some sort of sense. Detective Inspector Humphreys had given her a bag of sweets for killing little Willie. Father Donovan had given her three Hail Marys for killing little Willie and Evans the Bread. Three Hail Marys was a penance – not a very big penance – but a sign of disapproval for all that. It was wrong to kill, but not very wrong. You were completely forgiven for one death. You were mildly reprimanded for two. Provided you didn't exceed a reasonable quota, you weren't likely to get into serious trouble. Three Hail Marys equalled two deaths. Three Hail Marys equalled one lie (Dolly's). At first she had looked at Dolly with considerable curiosity. Had Dolly killed anyone? When had she had the chance – and who? It had become increasingly obvious that Dolly would have liked to dispose of Sister Philomena, but Sister Philomena was still around. And on being questioned Dolly had vigorously denied killing anyone. She had told a lie, she said; if she hadn't she'd have been stuck in the box with Father Donovan until they both dropped dead. Daft place – this. You had to go around committing sins just so as to please Father Donovan.

It hadn't seemed fair to Dolly that Zanny's horrific crimes should have been treated so leniently. The fact that Zanny was posh might have something to do with it. If she, Dolly, had made that sort of confession she would be in gaol this minute, being tortured. Sister Philomena was perhaps not such an enemy after all. Being polished up was a heck of a nuisance, but if you confessed your crimes in a prissy voice – like a blooming nightingale – then you got off. So, on her next visit to

Sister Philomena, she was unusually compliant. "Progress, dear child," Sister Philomena said, delighted, "is being made."

Progress in the next two years continued to be made. Dolly, on the surface, appeared acceptably middle-class. She even invented a nanny who had cared for her in her pre-kindergarten days. Those who didn't know her origins believed her. It amused her to speak of her dead parents as darling mummy and dearest daddy. Grandma Morton was: my wonderful grandmamma, now with God. And after two years' silence she probably was. Dolly still occasionally thought about her and grieved a little. In lonely moments she hugged her pillow in bed and buried her nose in it and tried to conjure up the smell of Grandma Morton – a normal smell of sweat and gin and a kind of distilled essence of affection. Birmingham had been real. Most of the time nastily real. The reality of the convent was less uncomfortable, but here you cried sometimes without knowing why. You wanted something, you didn't know what. A good biff across the ear-hole given by Grandma Morton or her mum and dad in the days of long ago had been a sign of caring. They might hate you like hell when they biffed you and you hated them back, but the emotion had its positive side, too. Here they liked you – mildly – or disliked you – mildly – and there wasn't any depth of feeling about any of it.

Zanny, too, was going through a passionless phase. Nothing here upset her very much. She couldn't do her sums, but could usually crib them from someone else. Had she been in the same class as Dolly she might have been jealous of Dolly's ability, but a good brain is not a commodity that can be wrenched from its owner. Dolly was able to keep her head and its contents in perfect safety.

Clare, who had aroused the nuns' ire for not having Dolly home for the holidays, began wondering if she might risk having her for a few days at a time. On the whole – better not. She was keeping her part of the bargain by paying her fees and buying her clothes and giving her presents on her birthday and at Christmas. If none of the children stayed in the convent during the holidays she would have been forced to take the risk, but several children spent the vacations there. For excellent reasons, Mother Benedicta had implied censoriously. My reason, Clare thought, is excellent plus. All the same, a day spent shopping in the county town with the two little girls could probably be accomplished safely. And the gesture would appease the nuns. Zanny would be aware of maternal affection that continued throughout term-time as well as during the holidays (well, dash it all, she did love her, didn't she?), and Dolly wouldn't feel too bereft. (A pity her grandmother hadn't turned up, but even if she did now it would, in the nature of things, be hello and goodbye.)

The day's outing passed without incident, apart from the air-raid sounding. They took refuge in a book shop because it happened to be handy and Clare gave them money to buy a book each. They both bought a film annual and in a rare moment of complicity assured Clare that the nuns wouldn't mind a bit. They were nice pictures. Tarzan was like a nature story – look at all those trees. Clare, looking at Johnny Weismuller's torso, wasn't deceived, but it was nice to see them grinning together. They seemed to be getting to like each other. Anyway the books were innocent. She began thinking of Peter. He was even less of a Tarzan than Graham. The war was going on too long. Graham was getting it somewhere, no doubt, or did constant carnage destroy the urge? If it didn't destroy the urge and you couldn't get it in the normal way – did you get it the other way? When Johnny came marching home would he have another Johnny in tow? It wasn't a pleasant thought. She repressed it.

It would have been wiser if Sister Clemence had

repressed a similar thought about her female charges. She was a forty-year-old French woman, ripely bosomed, who wore her nun's garb with fortitude rather than with enthusiasm. She intensely disliked dormitory duty but nevertheless approached it with unnecesssary zeal. Which was how she did everything. Instead of walking through the dormitory saying her rosary quietly to herself, or musing with sweet nostalgia about the days of her youth – long before Hitler and the war – her thoughts stayed firmly in the present. She did her duty to the letter and beyond. Lights went out at nine. Anyone having a late bath or a nocturnal visit to the lavatory had to get back into bed as best she could. Torches were not allowed. Whispered conversations over the white-boarded partitions of the cubicles were definitely not allowed. Clothes had to be folded neatly and placed on the chair at the bedside. Photographs of relatives – close relatives – might be displayed on the shelf by the wardrobe. Photographs of anyone else were prohibited. Clive Brook and Clark Gable appearing temporarily, and hopefully, as Daddy before he went to war might deceive some of her more naïve sisters in Christ, but not her. When Sister Clemence was on duty, pin-ups went under the mattress. Pages from Zanny's and Dolly's film books, torn out and exchanged for sweets, went under cover like the French resistance and travelled with some hazard from cubicle to cubicle. As the pages were limited in quantity, the girls travelled even more hazardously and viewed them under the blankets two to a bed. In the male-denuded landscape you protected your Franchot Tone and Melvyn Douglas from the eyes of malevolent authority by pushing them down to the bottom of the bed when Sister Clemence prowled by. If you were the visitor you took the torch with you and lay hopefully out of sight whilst the rightful owner of the cubicle feigned innocent sleep in full view of her prying eyes. After she had passed by you both got under the bed-clothes with your torch and your

56

film star and your world was full of men, beautiful men.

What was a Lesbian?

Why was Sister Clemence going up the creek?

Even the older girls thought her reaction to the crime was verging on paranoia. They were being sent to Ma Mère – for what? They were likely to be expelled – for what? Talking together in the dark? It didn't occur to them that the production of the pictures might put everything in a different light.

Sister Clemence shaking with emotion herded a dozen of them in their dressing-gowns down to Mother Benedicta's study and then went in search of higher authority.

Zanny and Dolly, the two youngest, looked at each other, bleary-eyed. What was she on about? They had been counting the remaining pictures and working out how many sweets they were worth. Their dressing-gown pockets were full of them. As vendors of the pictures they had been made much of by the older girls – and now thunder was breaking over their heads.

Mother Benedicta arrived in a fury and sent them all back to bed. She would see them in the morning, she said. She was a well-balanced woman who knew very well that Sister Clemence was not. If there was an explanation – not necessarily Sister Clemence's explanation – it would be found in the light of day.

She saw the girls, two by two. Lesbian partnerships, Sister Clemence called them. Mother Benedicta did not.

She began with the older ones and saw mystification rather than lust. If there was guilt, it wasn't guilt of the flesh. By the time she arrived at Zanny and Dolly she put the questions she had put to the others, but out of a sense of fairness and duty rather than of conviction.

"Zanny and Dolly, you were in bed together – why?"

"For company," said Dolly, who was the quick thinker.

"What were you doing?"

"Just lying there," said Dolly.

"And now, you answer me, Zanny – what were you doing?"

"Just lying there," said Zanny, taking her cue.

"Were you touching each other?"

How could you lie there in a three foot bed without touching?

"Yes," they chorused.

"Where did you touch?"

They both knew instinctively that they should not have touched. They didn't know why.

"Zanny's toe," Dolly said, "touched my toe."

"Dolly's left arm," said Zanny, "was squashed up against my neck."

"You didn't touch anywhere else?"

By the tone of the question it was highly undesirable to have touched anywhere else. What was she *talking* about?

This time they both chorused, "No."

She told them severely that it was a sin to break the school rules. The rule was that once you were in your own bed you stayed in it. You didn't leave your bed and get into another girl's bed for any reason at all. When they went to confession they would remember what they had done and tell Father Donovan.

On the whole, Dolly and Zanny decided, it would be better to tell Father Donovan that they had got in bed together to kiss. A kiss was the lightest of touches and quite obviously the sin was touching. The lie about kissing could be held over until the next confession as a handy sin in reserve.

He listened to them a little shaken – all the other confessions had been fleshless in implication – and told them to say the rosary through twice. And let the good Lord sort that one out, he thought. Mother Benedicta's cross, according to Mother Benedicta, was Sister Clemence and he was beginning to understand why. Individual sins confessed by the nuns and pupils linked up

together like a mosaic and that way you saw the convent as a whole. It was normal. It was human. He was
glad the Man Up There was the final arbiter. He, Father
Donovan, as the channel, was frequently relieved that
the buck could be passed. Indeed there were times, such
as now, when he couldn't get rid of it quickly enough.

To say the rosary through twice implied a sin of some
magnitude and once again Zanny's search for some sort
of moral guide was brought up short. Who planned all
these penances? Did Father Donovan have a book on it?
If she had put a pillow on Dolly's face and sat on it would
the penance have been three Hail Marys again – or
maybe four – or maybe five? Some sins were called
mortal and some were called venial. You went to hell for
the first lot. All her sins so far had been venial – and
murder was more venial than most. Murder didn't seem
to matter. Touching did. Her memory of little Willie
and the breadman was fading away like a lurid sunset
into the tender greyness of forgetfulness. Dolly, who
was pretending to say her rosary, dug Zanny with her
elbow and reverting to strong Midland for the sheer hell
of it said the whole set-up here was bleedin' daft. "Aint
no reason in any of it."

Zanny agreed.

From that moment she vowed never to look for a
reason again. There was no guide except the guide in
your own head. Sin was just a blob of quicksilver which
took on odd shapes and couldn't be pinned down. So get
rid of the concept. Chuck it out. Live. Her own words to
herself were simpler – for the most part she used no
words at all. She imagined herself sitting on a beach,
naked. The sun shone. There was no clutter. No fuss.
Her mind was like the inside of a shell. A mother-of-
pearl shell, pink and pretty, growing beautiful Zanny
pearls.

In 1945 on the day the war ended, Zanny had her first
period. The convent bells rang and the town bells rang

and streamers were thrown and everyone embraced everyone else with impunity. Zanny felt the warm wetness between her legs and shouted out with some astonishment and a degree of fright that she was a woman. Everyone was too pleased that Hitler's nose had been finally ground into the mud to take any notice. She fixed herself up with one of the sanitary towels that Mummy had provided and then lay on the bed waiting for momentous things to happen to her. It was an odd feeling being grown up (well, nearly eleven). There was a griping pain in her stomach and she seemed to be bleeding slowly to death. If this went on once a month until she was forty then somebody had it in for women. The extreme unfairness of it affronted her. Men should bleed, too. Daddy would be coming home soon. He hadn't bled at all. Not superficially, nor from any orifices. She was beginning to forget what he looked like.

Graham, who remembered Zanny as small, plump and lethal, was delighted with what he saw now. She'd be a corker one day when the puppy fat had fined down – it was already fining down around her waist. Her stomach no longer stuck out and she had little breasts which showed under her school blouse like inverted saucers. Not only was she a potential beauty, she was also good. The nuns had worked wonders with her. She hadn't killed anyone for years.

Unlike many of his compatriots he didn't find it at all difficult to settle down into family life again. His marriage wouldn't go bust. He took Clare to bed with the eagerness of a new lover and she received him with enthusiasm. Peter had become boring routine. Graham had new games to play. My cup, Clare thought, runneth over. The dark days have gone. Life, at last, is normal. Even normal enough to have Dolly to stay for a few days in the summer holidays. (Just a few days – don't push it.)

Graham, not over intelligent, was aware of Dolly's

intelligence without fully appreciating it. Her metamorphosis from a slum child into a well-spoken, perfectly acceptable young adolescent, took some getting used
to. He even called her Dorothy once or twice. She was
small, thin and gawky, not at all pretty. But her eyes
were good – they reminded him of the deep murky
brown of desert oases. If her eyelashes were real (well,
of course they were real), they were the best he'd
seen for a long time. She'd make play with those one
day.

But she didn't compare with Zanny. Fair, beautiful,
loving Zanny. There was no competing for affection.
Dolly, deliberately gauche at times, made sure of that.
She got asked out on holiday to several homes these
days and knew how to adapt. In the other homes she
adapted without any stress. Daddy – a major in the REs
– had been killed in El Alamein – one of Monty's lot.
That sort of thing. Occasionally he was a submarine
commander and had gone down at Dunkirk. Mummy, a
Wren officer – or a worker in Intelligence (I'm sorry I
don't know the details) – had either received a direct hit
or been liquidated. Her hosts, impressed or sceptical,
were polite and kind.

Here there was no fun or make-believe. Here there
was just a rather cautious present. She was grateful
that Zanny's parents were sufficiently guilt-ridden to
pay her fees and to look after her needs. She was wise
enough not to mention the reason – ever. The goldfish
pond had been filled in and made into a rockery full of
alpines. Grandma Morton wouldn't have approved of
those either. They should have been cabbages.

The convent garden, patriotically full of cabbages, tur-
nips and potatoes, had been tended during the war by
the nuns themselves, mostly by the lay sisters who,
with no money to bring into the Order, brought their
domestic and gardening skills while their better-
heeled, better-educated sisters brought their academic

abilities and their cash. All toil was offered to the greater glory of God – be it hoeing around the beetroot, doing the laundry, scrubbing floors, or teaching matriculation subjects to the sixth form.

With the ending of the war, the intake of pupils began to grow. During the following three years numbers rose to eighty. There was money enough now to refurbish the gardener's cottage and to employ a full-time gardener. Local gardeners, mostly ex-army, came and went. They were Welsh. They were not Catholics. The convent was a stop-gap. They put up with it – temporarily – as Mother Benedicta put up with them.

If she hadn't had to do so much putting-up she would have been wise enough not to have employed Murphy. Murphy, even in Mother Benedicta's convent-veiled eyes, was an extremely masculine animal. He was thirty years old. Irish. A Catholic. Extremely suitable apart from one thing – his overt masculinity. He wore an old flannel shirt and thick dirty corduroys and his body, thickset and muscular, shone through the lot like a promise of joy.

Clutching at straws, Mother Benedicta asked him if he were married – or likely to be married soon. He told her he wasn't and then grinned disarmingly and said that sure he'd had it in his thoughts, that he wasn't one of them quare ones, but he wasn't in any hurry to be rushing into marriage. If the nuns could be putting up with him – a single man – then he'd do the job just fine. He'd even raise rabbits for the convent table – there was room for hutches in the cottage back yard – and if he cleared the corner by the potting shed there'd be room for hens. The shed itself could house them. His enthusiasm was boundless. He had a tooth missing, top front left, and it was that rather than his zeal that won Mother Benedicta. He was flawed. Not much, but perhaps enough. Out of working hours, she told him, he would stay within the confines of his cottage and its garden. It had its own gate to the road. He wouldn't use the convent's main gates or take a short cut across the playing fields. For her part, she would see that the children didn't bother him. His cottage garden would be put out of bounds. If any of the girls played too close, or made a nuisance of themselves – by retrieving a ball, perhaps – he would send them packing immediately and report the incident to her.

He agreed to all this. A day walking through the streets of the county town, just a bicycle ride away, had shown him enough local talent to bed happily when the opportunity arose. Let old Mother Suspicious there isolate him like a leper, let her tack notices with Keep Out on them on the surrounding trees, sure he wouldn't quarrel with any of it. He told her so in different words.

Her fears were very slightly eased and she began bargaining over his salary. He didn't come cheap.

Neither did the temporary teachers who were useful stop-gaps until the mother convent in France could send over more nuns with the right teaching qualifications, but they were cheaper than employing certificated teachers. There were three of them. Twenty-year-old Robina Blane from Altrincham who wasn't sure if she wanted to teach or not and this was a good way of finding out. Bridget O'Hare, nineteen years of age and as Irish as the Liffey, who didn't mind having a bash, preferably at a tennis ball (she was taken on as sports mistress). And Miss Agatha Sheldon-Smythe who was bordering on retirement and needed a home for herself and her two pet budgerigars. Junior biology was her forte. The two young teachers shared a room near the convent infirmary. Miss Sheldon-Smythe had a bed-sitter on the ground floor near the library. Next to her budgerigars she had a deep regard for the Royal Family. When a member of royalty died, she donned complete mourning for a week. When they married or had a jubilee she wore a waistcoat of red, white and blue and put a flag on the budgies' cage. The girls liked her. She was pleasantly barmy. The nuns tolerated her; at least she knew her worms and could dissect frogs deftly and neatly.

Zanny and Dolly, now fourteen and fifteen, were in the senior school and in the efficient academic care of the nuns. Not that efficient academic care mattered much in Zanny's case. The only exam she had passed had been Junior Oxford and that by a fluke. The invigilator had slept peacefully throughout and she had been happily placed next to a class-mate with reasonable ability and a kind heart who didn't mind her copying. With Dolly, inefficient teaching would have mattered. She was quite obviously the most outstanding pupil the convent had had for years. She had the kind of quality that demanded quality. They saw her making Cambridge eventually and were quite prepared to see her through to her degree if the Moncriefs wouldn't. As an advertisement for academic success she would treble the intake.

The world was moving into a new era. The professional woman was coming into her own. In the pre-war days the girls were groomed for marriage. If they failed to ensnare a man by the age of twenty-five or so they ran genteel little boutiques, or tea-rooms specialising in home-made muffins, or they tended elderly relatives, or they became nuns. On the whole, Mother Benedicta thought, there was a great deal to be said for emancipation. If you had the choice of becoming an academician or a nun and you chose the latter then your vocation was truly based. God, in so many cases, had run a bad second to a reluctant lover or a failed exam. The number of nuns in the future might be depleted, but the quality and level of commitment should be superb.

That was more than could be said for the quality of Robina Blane or Bridget O'Hare. The former was finding out that she didn't want to teach anyway, but would stay for the summer term. Bridget wasn't too sold on teaching either, but she was sold on Murphy and nothing would prise her out while he was around. She

64

and Murphy shared roots. They spoke with the same soft southern accent. They were right for each other.

Murphy felt the same. He had once nearly married a girl like her with long dark hair, sturdy legs, and well rounded hips. When he looked at her he was reminded of buttermilk and brown eggs and a dash of the hard stuff to stop the sweetness, the wholesomeness, from cloying. She was a good mixture, this Bridget.

They spent evenings together in his little kitchen with the curtains drawn against the summer sunlight and prying eyes. They made love frequently, sometimes on the horsehair sofa (uncomfortable) but usually in the adjoining bedroom on an old-fashioned feather mattress (as comfortable as the fat bosom of Mother Ireland).

No wonder Bridget was too tired to teach the junior school basketball. As for tennis, she dreamed at the net and listened to the birds sing, while the balls whizzed past.

Zanny, too, had begun to dream. Her body, virgin ground, sent up little sensory tendrils of emotion that hardened her nipples. She didn't know what it was all about, but it happened when she thought of Murphy. When she sat in class pretending to listen to Sister Gabrielle talking about equilateral triangles and somebody called Pythagoras she could see him through the window tending the vegetable patch. On hot days he hung his shirt on the branch of an apple tree. His skin was darkly tanned and shone with sweat – like a chestnut with rain on it. The hair on his head was black, but on his chest it was a crisp nutty brown. She licked her lips, tasting Murphy, tingling to Murphy, and looked at Sister Gabrielle with glazed eyes when she called her to attention.

Most of her dreaming she did in the privacy of her bed. These summer nights the evening sun took a long time to die. The white, wooden partition of her cubicle became a pale gold, a soft ochre, and finally and brilliantly a deep rose before darkness fell. Though she had never spoken to him she carried on conversations with him in her mind. He told her she was beautiful. A colleen. (She knew he was Irish, so he probably used Irish words.) They danced together to the tune of "One Night of Love" played by a string orchestra and then he gave her a cocktail and invited her to dinner. He was rich now. His gardening period was therapy to get over a love affair. His uncle, a rich laird, (or was laird Scottish?) had died and left him his grouse moor. There was a castle on it – and a gazebo – and a maze. His bed was a four poster and he led Zanny to it very gently. She wore a pink nightdress with frills and a thing called a negligée over it with a border of swansdown. He told her that her feet were pink like the noses of the white angora rabbits he used to tend for the nuns in the convent a long time ago. He disrobed her and told her that her body was as white as their fur (or perhaps he didn't, that made her sound hairy and she wasn't, not more than normal and in the right places so alabaster was better – or white silk), and then he lifted her gently onto the bed.

At that point Zanny had an orgasm without knowing what it was. It had never happened to her before and she bit on the sheet and then stuffed a lot of it into her mouth to stop herself crying out. Being a woman was a most extraordinary thing. She turned on her side and imagined Murphy squashed up in bed with her. All that talk about touching being a sin and being punished with a couple of rosaries swam into her mind and then swam out again. If even not touching sent electric tremors through you that made your toes curl, what did touching do? She trembled at the prospect of finding out. This, then, was being in love. Oh, joy! Oh, Murphy!

Towards the middle of the summer term the convent celebrated its centenary. The Bishop came down and said Mass. He was a large jovial man who liked children

66

and played hide and seek with the young ones. When he left at the end of the day he ordered that the school should have a holiday spent in the way the girls liked best. Would they like a picnic? They would. On a beach? Yes, please. With lots of jammy cakes and sandwiches? Oh yes, Monseigneur.

It's all very well to beam like that, Mother Benedicta thought crossly. You don't have to arrange the jammy cakes and make sure that the school bus is serviced. You can't even persuade the Almighty to give us a nice day. On all the picnics in the past the weather had been devilish.

This year was devils' weather, too, for the lower and middle school (you couldn't transport eighty children on a massive picnic all at once), but for the upper school it was better. If there was enough blue in the sky to make a sailor a pair of trousers then you stood a chance of having a fine day. Today, Zanny thought, it will be all right. We won't come back cross, wet and bedraggled. She packed her bathing costume, a one-piece regulation one that did nothing for anybody, in her large white bath-towel, and went down to the bus feeling happy.

Murphy was in the driver's seat.

This was an unexpected bonus. Zanny instantly felt happier. She didn't know how it had been contrived. He was sitting there wearing a brown and white checked shirt with the sleeves rolled up. There were hairs on his arms running up from the wrists like a soft pelt. His fingers on the wheel were square, the nails a little spatulate and rimmed around with the black of honest toil (the grouse moor still to come). She could forgive him his nails. She could forgive him anything. She stopped on the top step of the bus and the hot sun burned her flesh, which was rather odd as it wasn't yet all that sunny.

Dolly kneed her from behind so that she was forced to move on. "Hope he's got his licence," Dolly said. Murphy

67

didn't impress her. In early childhood she had met many like him – Midland version. Nowadays she was beginning to like them smooth, if she gave them any thought at all.

There were four nuns in charge of the picnic party – and Bridget. As sports mistress it had been part of her duty to teach the girls swimming, not that she could swim very much, but she had played around with the younger ones in the convent swimming pool, splashed them and shown them how to float. On these picnic days, the venue was Coracle Bay, a small cove about twenty miles away and she was asked to go along and "keep an eye" as Mother Benedicta put it. Mother Benedicta herself had opted out. She had been on the first two picnics and done her fair share of settling her arthritic limbs on damp sand. A longish drive and a shortish period on the beach had been part of her strategy but shortish was still not short enough and she'd had her fill. She went into the coach to have a few words with Murphy before the children departed.

"You will remember," she said, "that your duty is to drive the girls to the picnic area – as you did yesterday and the day before – leave the coach so that they may return to it quickly if it should rain – and return to it yourself at four o'clock – earlier if it's wet." She didn't repeat the other instructions; that he should keep well away from the picnic party; that liquid refreshment in the form of tea or coffee could be taken at a small café in the village if his own flask of coffee wasn't sufficient; that he was on no account to go into any of the bars of the local hotels. Once, she hoped, had been enough.

Having driven with him twice she had no qualms about his driving ability. The school bus (donated by a retired colonel, the father of a third-former) was usually driven by Sister Sofia who had driven an ambulance during the war and knew what she was about. But Sister Sofia had unfortunately contracted shingles, and the other nuns who could drive cars drew the line at

68

coaches. Murphy, apprised of the situation by Bridget – and its convenience – had offered his services. When asked how he had known of the dilemma he had spoken fatuously about little birds and retrieved himself hastily by suggesting that the Almighty might have put it into his head. Mother Benedicta had eyed him suspiciously but was too bothered by the general hassle of the wretched picnic to question him any closer.

Murphy was glad she wasn't coming today. On the other two drives over to the picnic area old Mother Benedicta – old Mother Garrulous – had yapped about scenic beauty and the history of the area. A bit of a bore. Today the nuns were mercifully silent. One old biddy of about sixty was asleep with her mouth open. He re-angled his driving mirror so that he could see Bridget who was sitting three seats back. She caught his eye and winked at him. He grinned and honked his horn – beep – beepity – beep – beep. The girls chuckled and began to sing. No culture trip this – just fun, fun, fun.

He parked the bus as usual near the main beach and carried the heaviest hamper up the road towards the cove that Mother Benedicta had considered reasonably private. The girls and the nuns carrying what they could, trailed behind. Bridget, keeping a very tactful distance, brought up the rear. She was wearing a scarlet sweater and very short blue shorts and to hell with the nuns – this was nearly the mid twentieth century. In two years it would be 1950. "Roll out the Barrel", Bridget sang and Murphy in the lead heard her and took it up. The older nuns, ineffectual and embarrassed, tried to shush their charges as they sang lustily and pretended to roll about drunk.

It wasn't quite Zanny's scene. Did Murphy have to play a plebeian part with quite such enthusiasm? Perhaps he had. Perhaps it was all part of the act. His voice, a light baritone, thrilled her, but he was spoiling the image a little. She hadn't imagined him jolly. In her dreams he had been imbued with a grave dignity. They

69

had walked together under palm trees on the white sand of a tropical beach. He had worn a tuxedo with a carnation in the button-hole. Before going to bed, (they always went to bed), he had brought a bottle of champagne into the bedroom. It was half buried in a bucket of ice. When he uncorked it the champagne shot out like the Niagara falls and soaked her nightdress (turquoise blue satin). He removed it, laughing. Then what followed was usually up to Zanny.

"Run, Rabbit, Run," Murphy bellowed. They had reached the cove now and had to climb over a small wall and go across slippery grass to get to it. He helped all the nuns over. The older ones gave him their hands disapprovingly. The younger ones pretended to disapprove, but nevertheless followed suit. The girls sprinted over athletically apart from one pretty little creature with hair like honey who insisted on being helped. He could have sworn she made a little scratching movement on the middle of his palm with her index finger. She had certainly blushed. Her cheeks had been almost the colour of Bridget's sweater.

He had a few quiet words with Bridget, after putting the picnic baskets on the beach, and then took himself off. He had his own small picnic basket packed by one of the lay sisters and with "Murphy" written on a label tied to the handle. He ate his sandwiches on the main beach. There was a wind blowing in from the sea and there were just a few families dotted around trying to huddle away from it. The local schools weren't on holiday yet. Mother Benedicta – Mother Vigilant – could have had the picnic here easily enough – there was plenty of room for everyone and it was a better beach. He lay on his back and snoozed for a while. The weather began to warm up a little.

Dolly, too, lay on her back, bored and rather chilly. She had had her duty swim because the nuns made a heck of a fuss if you didn't. Had she thought of it in time she could have said she had the curse. "I've got the curse, dear sister, dear sister, dear sister, I've got the curse, dear sister, dear sister, the curse." She sang quietly to herself. What was supposed to be so therapeutic about going into a cold – very cold – sea, and then coming out and not being able to dry yourself properly? Her flesh was still damp. There was damp sand all down her thighs. Why didn't she have decent thighs like Zanny? Zanny Fatty – only not so fatty any more. When Zanny grew up she'd probably be a whore. Well, there wasn't much else she could be and the money was good. She dreamed about Zanny whoring it up in the West End, (she'd never been to London, but the West End sounded the right sort of locality). Zanny dripping with diamonds in a white Rolls-Royce.

And what about herself? The nuns seemed quite determined to shove her into university. Not that she'd mind, but Zanny's mum and dad wouldn't keep doling out cash for ever. There were times when she wouldn't mind swopping her brain for Zanny's bosom. Zanny academically was a dead duck, but looking the way she did it didn't matter.

Dolly leaned up on her elbow to see what Zanny was doing. But she wasn't there.

Zanny was sitting half way up the scree on the far side of the cove where an outjutting rock formed a windbreak. Here it was comfortable and reasonably warm. She had told Sister Gabrielle that she was going in search of wild flowers and that she wouldn't be long. She had gathered some sea thrift and they lay papery and pink in her lap. The sea was lonely. There was a poem about the lonely sea and the sky. The girls down on the beach were sitting around in groups, a few were playing with a large beach ball. She could see Dolly lying on her own with a book. Dolly would read her way through life and never live it. Well, she couldn't live it very much looking like that. Okay – so she fluttered her eyes at Daddy – and Daddy ogled back like an idiot. But to get on in life you needed more than eyes. She'd get a degree in the end probably, and finish up teaching equilateral triangles and the co-efficients of linear expansion to those fool enough to listen . . . or she'd be a nun.

It must be hell, Zanny thought, to be a nun.

She looked down at the picnic party on the beach again. Nobody was looking up at her. It would be perfectly safe to walk into the village and see if Murphy were around. She imagined the conversation if she met him. "Mr. Murphy, I'm so glad I bumped into you. I need to get into the coach. I've left something inside it, you see."

"Good afternoon, young lady, how fortunate we should have met. I noticed you in the coach, naturally, on the drive over. In fact I made some enquiries about you – your name is Miss Moncrief, is it not?"

"Well – yes. My Christian name is Zanny – do please use it."

"How nice of you. My Christian name is . . ."

But she couldn't think of a suitable one. For once she was stymied. He was Murphy. Beautiful – suave – poised – hard-fleshed – bubbling with fiery emotion (now held in check) Murphy. So scrap that last bit of dialogue.

They would be in the coach now to find what she had left in it. What had she left in it? A perfumed handkerchief? No – too ordinary. A book of poetry? To dull. A French letter? What was a French letter? She had heard of it but didn't know what it was. It sounded just right.

"As a matter of fact, Mr. Murphy, a French letter – under the seat."

It would probably be gone – whatever it was. He would commiserate.

He would suggest, perhaps, that they might have a cup of tea in that café over there. He might at this moment be in that café over there. She went over to it and opened the door and looked inside. A family with four children were eating ice-cream. No Murphy.

72

She spent some little while walking through the village and then went up into the dunes. The sand here was very thick and dry and filled her sandals. The wind was cut off and the hollows were hot. It was a pity people threw orange peel into them. This was a very beautiful bay. One day in the future she and Murphy would come back together, a nostalgic return to the place of their first meeting. "My dear," he would say, "do you remember that day in the dunes? Your hair was like liquid gold, my dearest. Do you know, that was when I fell in love with you?"

The dialogue was becoming just a little stilted. Her nightly imaginings were quite a lot better – much more sophisticated. He had never used the word love – just looked it and held her.

Where was he? Perhaps on that headland over there. He would be sitting gazing out to sea – as she had been doing earlier. If she were making a film of this the cameras would pan from one to the other and then they would both get up slowly and do that kind of odd slow waltz towards each other that the film people managed so well. There would be music – a violin.

Drat the sand! She had to keep taking her sandals off and emptying them. She went back onto the road again until she was nearer the headland and then got over the wall and found a path through gorse bushes. This was a high, wild place. Quite close the sea crashed into an inlet. She could hear it but not as yet see it.

She saw Murphy before she saw the sea. There was a black area of burnt gorse surrounded by bushes that hadn't been burnt. On the burnt floor of his bed was a white school regulation towel. On the towel was Bridget, naked from the waist down. On top of Bridget, also naked in the same region, was Murphy.

Zanny hadn't seen the act before, but she knew what it was all about. Trembling with shock she went down on her knees and crawled away very carefully through a narrow entry into a deep cave of gorse. It was an animal's lair of some sort and now served well as her hiding place. She didn't cry. This went beyond tears. Pain was splitting her in two. She crouched there moaning.

Murphy and Bridget, too engrossed in their lovemaking to attune their ears to the outside world, heard Zanny moan but didn't pay any attention. The sea was making a racket down there and there were animals around and birds – a sea-gull could have been spewing up something, or a rabbit could have been disturbed by a stoat. As far as they knew there were no humans around. Before making love they'd had a humdinger of a row. They often had. A row was a good stimulus. This time it was about Charles Parnell. Murphy had called him a bastard for reasons he couldn't now remember. Bridget had been stormy in his defence. Modern Irish politics in this period immediately following the war weren't particularly stimulating, but you could always have recourse to the past. An on-going peace was unnatural, just as a totally peaceful, loving relationship was unnatural. Bridget wouldn't have scratched him so passionately during the act of love if she hadn't spat at him in anger a short while before it.

He got off her, grinning.

She wiped the blood on his shoulder with her finger. There were lots of things she had to tell this man, this lover of hers, and lots of things she wouldn't tell him. The time of choosing was getting rather close. Why, in the name of God, be a gardener in a convent? That was his trouble – lack of ambition. Why not raise rabbits and hens in the backyard of a nice little pub – somewhere on the west coast, perhaps? She had always fancied Connemara.

"You are a good man," Bridget said, comparing him with someone he knew nothing about.

"Not at all bad at it," said Murphy modestly, not understanding.

He wished he could spend the rest of the afternoon out

here with Bridget. So did she, but other responsibilities beckoned. She'd have to get back to the nuns and the children soon. Children? Adolescent girls, this lot. Quivering in Murphy's presence like harp strings briskly plucked.

"You have very sexy hands," she said, "but you should clean your dirty finger-nails."

He liked the compliment about his hands. Of course they were sexy. He knew how to use them. As for his nails being dirty, they'd be dirtier still in a minute. One of the off-side wheels of the bus needed attention. It had better be seen to now.

He pulled on his trousers and told Bridget to give him ten minutes. She'd need that anyway to get herself tidied up.

Zanny, from her lair, watched him go. She had heard him say ten minutes. Her time was short. She crept out of the bushes, feeling cold and sick. The pain in her flesh and in her bones slowed her like sudden senility. She had to force her limbs to move. The place had to be reconnoitred for the right spot. And for the right weapon. At last she found both.

Gently, plaintively, she began to call out. "Miss O'Hare – Miss O'Hare."

Bridget, fastening the button of her shorts, looked up startled. The voice seemed to be coming from over the ridge where the sound of the sea was loud. She bent over and fastened her sandals and then went to look.

The pretty one – Zanny something or other – was crouching over something in the slippery grass. She was dangerously near the edge.

"Whatever you've got there," Bridget said sharply, "leave it and come back up here." (How much had the girl seen? Damn her!)

"Oh, but I can't," Zanny said plaintively, "I think it's dying."

"What is dying?"

"A dear little creature. A dear little soul." (Willie in

75

heaven picking apples for Jesus. Evans the Bread burning up a tree.)

"A *what?*" Despite her better judgment, Bridget went to look.

As she leaned over, Zanny brought the lump of granite down hard on the back of her neck and then gave her a shove. Half-concussed, Bridget slid several feet down the slope, scrabbled at the rough earth at the top of the cliff, and then sailed in a perfect crimson and blue arc downwards and into the evil green of the sea below.

It wasn't the most spectacular death of the three – it couldn't compare with Evans the Bread – but for Zanny it was the most satisfying. She sat for a little while looking down into the gully while the sea creamed like dirty lace around Bridget's long dark hair.

Three

W hen the bus didn't arrive until very late Mother Benedicta knew something was wrong. Her first thought was that Murphy had got drunk and crashed it. She had never seen him drunk, but she had sensed that her warning to keep away from the temptation wasn't maligning him. When the bus eventually ground up the convent drive at nearly half past nine she went to meet it.

Murphy, at the wheel, was white with suppressed rage, but there wasn't a whiff of the hard stuff near him. He had searched for Bridget for a long time. Eventually he had seen someone who had looked like Bridget – she had worn a crimson jersey and shorts – getting into a dinghy with a couple of yachtsmen. At a distance he could hear their laughter. One of the sods had his arm around her waist. That she should ditch him so blatantly for a bloody toff with a sailing boat had made his Irish ire explode. He had gone back to the nuns and the girls who were waiting anxiously and told them that he had seen her and that she could bloody walk. She could run screaming after the bus, he said, and he hoped her bleeding feet would drop off. Though he had been reasonably restrained (he could have put it much more colourfully), the nuns took it badly. And one of the girls got sick. Right there on the floor. He thought she was going to pass out, but she didn't. She was the pretty one. The sexy one he'd helped over the wall. One of the nuns mopped up the mess and another one gave her a barley sugar to settle her stomach. She sat and crunched it and looked at him, her eyes wide with horror.

Most of this was told to Mother Benedicta by various members of the party. Zanny's sickness they attributed to sensitivity. They had no idea that Murphy's words had conjured up a ghoul climbing bloodily out of the gully, like Dracula out of a tomb, and shrieking vengeance as it sped after the bus on its route – its very fast route – back to the convent. Mother Benedicta, attributing it to physical causes – too many sandwiches perhaps – told Zanny to spend the night in the infirmary. If she were to be sick again she had better do it there.

As for Bridget O'Hare, girls of nineteen didn't behave with much sense unless they were novices or postulants – and not even then – and if she chose to have a night out then it was probably better not to advertise the fact. When she returned in the morning she would have her marching orders. It would be quite stupid, at this stage, to call the police.

She told the girls to go to bed as quietly as they could and not to wake anyone in the dormitory. They could for this once say their prayers quietly in bed. If anyone wanted milk she could help herself in the refectory – also biscuits – but not to linger over it.

"I hope," she said crossly, "that despite everything, you enjoyed your day."

"Oh yes, Ma Mère," they chorused, and with a degree of truth. The picnic had been memorable – quite how memorable they were yet to find out.

When Bridget hadn't returned by eleven o'clock the following morning, Mother Benedicta, with great reluctance, phoned Sergeant Thomas of the local police. She asked for him personally. He had recently dealt with a case of bicycle vandalism – the removal of pumps and pedals from four bicycles belonging to the younger, more athletic, nuns. She had liked his style. He hadn't joked about it. His subordinate had been facetious about the pedals, whereas Sergeant Thomas had taken it very seriously. He was up at the convent within the hour. His gravity, this time, was perfectly in keeping with what he had to say.

She wouldn't throw hysterics, he knew. She wouldn't scream, or shout. Even so, he had to lead in with some finesse. He couldn't throw the news at her like hurling an old boot. You didn't treat nuns like that.

The body had been found just after seven-thirty by a local resident out walking her dog along the cliffs who had happened to look down into the gully. At first she hadn't connected the splash of red with a body held about two feet under the surface of the water by a tangle of black hair. When she eventually began believing in what she was looking at, she informed her husband, the coastguards and the police, in that order. Everyone had moved with commendable speed.

The description that had been circulated fitted exactly with Mother Benedicta's description of the missing school teacher. Identification would be easy, too. If her hair hadn't trapped her – hair like a rope, she had – she would this moment be tossing like a cork in the Irish sea. The sea liked to play with its victims, but this time it had been baulked. There had not been enough strength in it to force her out of the rocks. No gale yesterday, nor last night. Like an old woman the sea had been, arthritic and slow.

"Well, now, Mam," he said gently, "drowning is always a possibility."

"You mean you've found her?" Though shocked, Mother Benedicta spoke incisively.

He soothed. "Maybe – maybe not. We've found a body – sounds like your gel." He read her the description on the circular and Mother Benedicta nodded.

They were both standing in the middle of the parlour and Mother Benedicta had the table behind her. The maidenhair fern – it was always maidenhair fern – touched her clenched hands which she held behind her back. If a fern could caress, then this fern caressed. Gently – gently – a voice at the back of her mind seemed to say. Take it easy now. In the name of the Father, the Son . . . the thought trailed away.

"A nice cup of tea," Thomas suggested, "and lots of sugar?"

Oh no, she wouldn't pass out, this Mother of the convent, this stiff-backed lady, but right this minute she could do with a little help. He knew where the bell was and presumed to ring it. She allowed him temporarily to take charge.

Later, in complete command of herself again, she told him Murphy's story about the yachtsmen. It puzzled him, but he couldn't discredit it. According to his colleagues, the body had probably fallen down into the gully and been trapped on impact with the rocks below. Nobody had said anything about a yachting disaster. But there hadn't been time to say much about anything. He decided to have a word or two with Murphy and asked where he might find him.

"Going about his duties," Mother Benedicta said crisply, "in the kitchen garden." She offered to accompany him, but he declined. Although he didn't know where the kitchen garden was, he wanted to see Murphy on his own.

Zanny, too, wanted to see Murphy on her own. Sister Agnes, who was a SRN and totally bored with her occasional duties with children who were mildly sick, had greeted her in the infirmary without much enthusiasm. An upset stomach was best starved. An upset psyche, though obvious in this case, she attributed to an upset stomach. Zanny went to bed supperless and the night was almost through before she slept. The rational explanation – that Murphy had seen someone else, not Bridget bloodily dead – had come to her slowly. But why had he been so angry? What had this other person who looked liked Bridget been doing? Why had he stormed back to the bus in such a rage? Had he come across the other Bridget making love? If he had come across the live Bridget making love would he have thrown her over the cliff? If so, then wasn't it a good thing that she, Zanny, had done it for him?

Wouldn't he eventually – one day – be pleased?

She imagined the two of them a long time in the future when they were both quite old – fifty at least. They were sitting on the sea-front at Monte Carlo – or was it Cannes? He had a white walking stick between his knees and he was resting his chin on it. He was blind. He had become blind when, like Rochester, he had been temporarily unfaithful to her and later, repenting, had put his lover's house on fire. Well, maybe she had got the story a bit wrong, but something like that. Anyway, he had disposed of his mistress and had become blind in the process. "My dear love," he told her, "my dear Zanny, you were always too good for me." "Oh, Murphy," she replied (what *was* his first name?), "oh, darling – if you only knew." At that point she would tell him about Bridget. His face would brighten with joy that she, too, had sinned. He wouldn't use the word, of course. It was pretty well obsolete in her vocabulary, too. But he would say something like: "You're so human, my love. So warm. So passionate. So *honest*."

But there was no point in being honest yet. She would just feel around – try to find out how he was taking it. It was conceivable that he might even have liked Bridget, though according to Dolly men did that sort of thing with women as a kind of reflex action. Dolly's knowledge of the world must have been learned from all the books she read – or else her memory went back a long time. To another age, perhaps. Dolly in the seventeenth century would have sold charm cures to victims of the plague and grown rich. A born survivor, Dolly. She had looked at her very oddly when she had been sick in the bus. It was a pity her parents were lumbered with her. They had been lumbered with her now for nearly ten years. A tenth of a century.

Zanny, at that point, had turned on her side and gone to sleep. Mathematics always had that effect on her. Bridget in the dark sea became an octopus gently fingering long green weed. Murphy, bright-eyed, cast a line into the water and tickled the probing fingers. They curled and gripped and then fell away softly one by one. Total darkness descended.

For Zanny to see Murphy on her own was about as difficult as getting an audience with the Pope – or getting out of Alcatraz. Possible, of course, all things are possible, but requiring a lot of thought.

Sergeant Thomas had no difficulty at all. Murphy was digging potatoes. The man had a lot of muscle, Thomas noticed with envy. That spade he was wielding was a good weight. The potatoes were a good weight, too. He grew Edzell Blue himself and sometimes Red Craigs Royal. These that Murphy was digging were white fleshed. "Pentland Dell?" he asked.

Murphy, who hadn't heard him approach, swung round in surprise. The names of potatoes were far from his mind and then he made the connection. He didn't know what they were called. He pushed in tubers – they grew – he dug them out – the lay sisters cooked them.

"I like a good turnip myself," Thomas went on conversationally, "especially Green Top Stone . . . Saw Bridget O'Hare with some yachtsmen, did you?"

Murphy put down the spade. Anxiety had been growing in his stomach during the night like a vegetable with blight on it.

Thomas wasn't in uniform, but police had their own peculiar smell. Very antiseptic. You touched them with rubber gloves. You were polite.

"Yes, sorr," he said, rolling his r's in agitation.

"She's dead," Thomas dropped the information like a Nazi bomb and waited curiously to see what devastation he had caused – if any.

Shock tends to hold one immobile, like a rag of ether over the face. Murphy's skin became pallid and then after several minutes flushed. He went and sat on the low stone wall that separated the kitchen garden from his cottage.

"What did they do," he asked, "drown her?" (They

82

made love in the boat, maybe, and capsized it?) He dug the nail of his right thumb into the flesh of his left thumb to see if he could feel anything. He couldn't.

Cool bastard, Thomas thought, who had missed the pallor, the flush, and heard only the voice – very level.

"What makes you think," he asked gently, "that the poor little gel was drowned?"

Murphy was beginning to feel. He kicked at some groundsel at the base of the wall and then gouged it out with the toe of his boot. They must have capsized it – the bloody inefficient yobs. He should have stopped them taking it out to sea. He should have gone over to them and ripped their balls off.

The Welsh policeman was looking at him pretty hard. The normal affinity between the Welsh and the Irish thinned in the gaze. Murphy, trying to regain some sort of emotional equilibrium, said the first thing that came into his head.

"Groundsel," he said, "for Miss Sheldon-Smythe's budgerigars."

"Oh?" said Thomas, surprised.

Murphy picked up a couple of roots of it, shook off the soil, and put the groundsel on the wall beside him. Dirty finger-nails, Bridget had said. There were thick smears of soil over his halfmoons. Her nails were like filberts – bright red with polish. His blood had been wiped off by her soft white finger. When they had made love. He liked the old-fashioned way of describing it. Love. A smell of burnt gorse. A white towel.

Thomas joined him on the wall. "Why drowned?" he asked again.

"They went in a boat, didn't they?" asked Murphy.

"I don't know. Did you see them going in a boat?"

"They were getting into a boat."

"You didn't watch while they went out to sea?"

"No." He had been too crazy with rage. He had assumed they had gone out to sea.

"Are you trying to tell me, sorr," he asked, still on the

83

surface commendably calm and exceedingly polite, "that she was not drowned?"

Thomas picked up a piece of the groundsel. Did birds eat this stuff? "Oh, yes," he said, "she was drowned all right – poor little gel. By that I mean the water got into her lungs. But she might have been knocked unconscious before it did, if you see what I mean."

"You mean," Murphy was aghast, "that she was *murdered*?"

"Oh, no," Thomas soothed. "Oh, no, no, no. Not necessarily – not necessarily at all. She was found in a gully under water. The grass on the clifftop is very slippy. She might have got too close to the edge. On her face she fell. Hair between two rocks. Got held there. Lots of possibilities, of course. How many yachtsmen did you see?"

Murphy didn't hear the question. His head felt like a witch's cauldron. It boiled, it bubbled, it seethed, it threw up obscene scraps of carrion. And then it calmed down.

Thomas was repeating the question.

"I don't know, sorr – two, mebbe three."

"What were they doing?"

"One of the sods had his arm around Bridget."

This time Thomas skimmed off some of the emotion from the top of the cauldron and gave it a good hard look. Oh, well, it wasn't surprising. It occurred to him that Murphy might be the best choice to make the identification – a preliminary identification – before her parents were informed. They would identify her officially, of course. Mother Benedicta had offered to go along. She could still go, and sit in the car: if it turned out not to be Bridget she wouldn't be subjected to an unnecessary ordeal. The enquiry as from now would be pushed up the line a bit. As sergeant he hadn't all that much authority.

He put his thoughts to Murphy. "If my superiors okay it – and if Mother Benedicta agrees – would you be willing to go to the mortuary to identify her?"

Yes, Murphy said, he would be willing. He would need to change his suit. He had a navy-blue serge one, would that do?

No need for a chapel suit, Thomas told him, in these circumstances. Just a clean pair of boots, maybe, and trousers with no mud on them.

Murphy went into his cottage to get himself ready just in case. He ran the hot tap in the sink but the water wasn't hot enough so he put it in the kettle to boil. When it boiled he couldn't remember what it was boiling for. He raised the kettle high and poured it away. It steamed around his face and got into his eyes. When he and Bridget had bathed each other it had taken four kettlesful to make the water in the tin bath warmer than tepid. She had made fun of his sulphur soap.

He stood very still in the middle of the kitchen and then he threw his head back and all the pain that was rolling around inside him came out as a mighty roar.

Thomas, half way across the lawn, heard something that sounded like a trapped animal. There wouldn't be any snaring around here – very pretty these convent gardens – very civilised. He must have imagined it. It wouldn't happen here.

"It's time," Graham told Clare, "that you and I – both – forgot what should have been forgotten a long time ago."

They were sitting at the breakfast table. They were not eating breakfast. The eggs and bacon were congealing on their plates. The morning newspaper was on the floor.

"It is time," he repeated, "to put it out of our minds."

Since the war he had managed to put a great deal out of his mind. Most of the unpleasant tapes that had run through the recorder during the last few years he had successfully wiped clean. This particular tape – this Zanny tape – had lost some of its clarity, but it refused to be destroyed. It had lain at the back of the drawer –

85

semi-forgotten – and now there it was again, louder and clearer than ever.

In the shape of a paragraph in the local weekly.

"Tragic Death of Young School Teacher" was the heading in heavy type, and underneath in small print: "Whilst on a school picnic the death occurred very tragically of Miss Bridget O'Hare (nineteen), a school teacher at the local convent. She was accompanying the senior girls on a day's outing to Coracle Bay. It seems that after spending some while on the beach she went for a stroll on the cliffs, just a few minutes walk away from the venue of the picnic. The following morning her body was found in a ravine at the base of the cliffs. An autopsy is being carried out. Much sympathy is felt for her parents and for the Mother Superior at the convent."

"Zanny," he pointed out, clutching at straws, "is not a senior girl. She is fourteen."

Clare removed the straw. "The senior school starts at fourteen. Zanny moves up automatically whether she passes exams or not. And she did pass the last one. Somehow. Are you going to eat your bacon?"

"No."

"Neither am I."

Clare removed both plates to the kitchen and then brewed up fresh coffee. She wished her hands would stop shaking. She wished Graham wouldn't keep trying to console her with his voice while his eyes plainly begged her to console him. He was forty now and looking it. This morning he looked older.

Earlier they had had a row about contraception. She was thirty-six, he said, and her reproductive days would soon be over. To leave things any longer would be dangerous. Dangerous – that was a laugh!

"If we had a son," she said, returning with the coffee, and to the original cause of the argument, "he'd probably have two heads with horns on them."

"Zanny is a perfectly nice, normal, young girl." He wished she wouldn't exaggerate everything. He wished he could believe that Zanny was a perfectly nice, normal, young girl. He did, most of the time. Most of the time she was a delight. He was immensely proud of her. Most of the time.

"It's lucky," she said, "that today is Saturday."

"Why?"

"You don't have to go to the office."

Although quite a successful accountant, he preferred days that were not working days. But why state the obvious? Clare's remark however was not quite as banal as it sounded. "We could," she said, putting a sweetener into her coffee, "go and see her."

"See Zanny – why?"

"Well – just pay a visit."

"It's the middle of term – we can't just pay a visit."

"I've done it before – when you were in Africa. I took her and Dolly shopping."

"Why?"

She couldn't remember why. She remembered the air-raid, though, and the bookshop. "Just to see they weren't homesick, I suppose."

"They were little more than babies then. They're grown up now – nearly. If we lived a long way off we could drop in – on our way somewhere else. You can't drop in when you're just a few miles away. Not unless you have something of importance to say."

(Such as: Zanny, did you or did you not murder Miss Bridget O'Hare?) They both asked the question in their minds.

"There's always the piano," Clare said.

"What?" He wondered if anxiety were driving her mental.

She was brightening up. "You know when I sold the old one I vowed I wouldn't have another – that it took up too much room. Zanny never touched it, but even so, she made a fuss. Well – we could have a new one."

He didn't follow her. What had all this to do with Zanny now?

87

"It's a good reason to see her," Clare explained. "We'll go to the convent and ask her if she'd like a new piano for her fifteenth birthday next month. We've had an offer of one, we'll say. Second-hand, but expensive. We don't want to buy it unless she'll practise on it."

"A piano? Couldn't we make it a violin – a flute – a mouth-organ . . . by God! A piano!"

"It has to be expensive enough to give the visit some *point*. Surely you see that? If you can think of a better reason for going – then tell me."

Mother Benedicta, heavily weighted by present events, received the Moncriefs politely. It was something about a piano and about Zanny being musical. When children tended to be weak academically parents sometimes compensated in other directions. It wasn't a bad thing. She hoped Zanny would say yes to the piano. An expensive outlay, certainly, even though second-hand. Was the Moncrief money perhaps a little tight? She hoped not – for Dolly's sake. She was pleased they wanted to see Dolly, too. She had never been able to understand why they hadn't taken to her more lovingly. That tale about jealousy long ago was really quite irrelevant now. They weren't bosom friends by any means, but there had never been any overt hostility. Dolly should spend her holidays with Zanny in the Moncrief home. Other families received her at holiday time with much pleasure. She was a pleasant, intelligent girl. As nice as Zanny.

Oh to God that Bridget O'Hare had been as intelligent.

"We were so sorry," Graham said, perhaps with more feeling than was necessary, "to hear about the young teacher."

"The will of God," Mother Benedicta said, not wholly believing it, but it was a good phrase that revealed nothing. The best way to deal with death. She didn't want to talk about it.

88

"A terrible accident," Clare probed fearfully.

"I'll see that the two girls are sent to you," Mother Benedicta said, "and some tea and cakes will be brought in at four. You will excuse me if I can't stay and enjoy your company, but I have some rather pressing duties."

The O'Hare parents needed some hand-holding. They were over in the visitors' annexe and were behaving as any normal parents would behave in these shocking circumstances.

"What a nice problem," she said, departing, "the purchase – or otherwise – of a piano."

Snide, Clare thought. Definitely sarcastic. A threat of greater problems to come, perhaps.

Zanny, like Mother Benedicta, was mildly astonished by the reason for her parents' presence. She kissed her mother and hugged and kissed her father. Dolly cautiously shook hands with both and raised her face to be kissed. She didn't kiss back. When Graham squeezed her hand she let it stay limp.

She was living now in a carefully guarded little cell of self-preservation. At times the situation amused her. At times it appalled her. On the whole, though, she thought she could handle it. She had no doubt at all about the real reason for the Moncriefs' visit. The local papers were left in the hall for the staff to collect, it was always possible to have a quick dekko before they did.

They were sitting in the parlour: it was like a scene from a Jane Austen novel. Conversation was being politely bounced about. "You're looking a little pale, Zanny dear, are you sure you're taking your extra orange juice every morning?" "Oh, Mummy, I'm fine." "You're taking it, of course, Dolly? You really are looking very well, dear. I'm sure you've grown nearly an inch since I saw you last."

And Mr. Moncrief (Graham as she thought of him), chipping in with pleasant, fatuous remarks about the treat the local boys would have when the two lovely ladies eventually left school.

In a minute, Dolly thought, we will drink tea. The tray will be placed on the table after Sister Bernadette has removed the fern. We will eat sandwiches of chicken paste and the cake will be a slab cake with cherries and currants.

She was right in every respect.

And now, she thought, after she delicately removed a crumb from her lip, the Moncriefs will get down to business. She couldn't help feeling rather sorry for them. They really were rather nice. Especially Graham.

"Well," Clare said, rather desperately, "the piano is settled, then. You definitely want it?"

"I don't much mind," said Zanny. She wondered if Murphy were musical. The Irish were good on the violin, weren't they? They called it the fiddle. They played jigs. Murphy had a sense of humour – he let his dignity slip a little now and then – he might, just for fun, play a few reels. But most of the time he'd play something slow and sad like "The Londonderry Air". "Oh, Danny Boy" – the pipes – the pipes are calling. He'd sing it in that lovely baritone of his and the tears would come to her eyes . . . as they were coming now.

Mummy was looking very worried. "Zanny, you're all right, aren't you?"

"Of course I am." (Why did she have to interrupt her dream just then? The only place where you could have a decent day-dream here without interruption was in bed – and then you tended to fade off into sleep.)

"She wasn't all right after the picnic," Dolly said, "she got sick in the bus."

A simple remark. A small crackle like distant thunder. A harmless striking of the dust in the region of Zanny's feet – a bullet carefully aimed. A warning. No blood. Yet.

Zanny looked at Dolly and then she looked at her parents. "Picnic food here," she said coolly, "is not as good as your picnic food, Mummy. I think the chicken paste was off."

"Is that why you went off – a little while after Miss O'Hare went off – because you weren't feeling well?"

Dolly's sabre, now unsheathed, gleamed in the afternoon sunlight. She passed the plate of cakes to Clare. Clare, frozen into silence, shook her head mutely.

Graham, who already had a piece, took another. He didn't know what kind of jungle maze he was walking through, but this was, indeed, jungle.

Zanny answered Dolly's question, her eyes a little narrowed. The sleeper was no longer asleep, then? How long had she been awake? How much had she seen?

"I went off," she said, "to pick flowers. I wasn't sick until we were all in the bus and ready for the drive back."

"Oh, yes," Dolly said cheerfully, "I remember. Murphy was in a towering rage about not finding Bridget O'Hare, wasn't he? He said she could walk back. And then you got sick."

"He said he had seen her," Zanny pointed out. "Don't forget that."

Dolly took a polite sip of tea. "Well, of course," she said. "Why wouldn't he have seen her? What was so surprising that he should have seen her? I mean – why mention that now?"

Zanny, casting around for an answer, couldn't find one. Everyone except Dolly stopped eating. Dolly, gloriously hungry, wonderfully elated, saw her own future mapped out in clear and perfect detail. An academic life could be dull, but it could also scintillate. She saw her chance. Now was the time to construct the foundation, brick by careful brick.

"It was a very unfortunate picnic," she told Graham and Clare. "Bridget O'Hare got killed. Murphy – he's the gardener here, but he drove the bus – was so angry when she didn't return that he drove back like a lunatic. Zanny looked awful. Of course we didn't know that Bridget had been killed until the following day. Murphy said he'd seen her, but he must have seen someone else. Well, we'll know the facts one day, I suppose. Do you know, this cake isn't at all bad, the cherries are quite juicy."

Graham put his plate on the table. If Clare's stomach felt anything like his, it would appreciate a stiff whisky. He didn't dare look at her, neither did he look at Zanny. He had been in court once, accused of a minor motoring offence. There had been no barrister – no judge – just a collection of local JPs. He was beginning now – in Dolly's presence – to appreciate what the atmosphere of a criminal court could be like. He met her eyes briefly. Where along the line had she shrugged off her familiar rather jokey identity? What was she now, for God's sake? What did she want from them?

"Mother Benedicta," Dolly said, picking it up telepathically, "is rather keen that I should learn Greek. It's not on the curriculum. Latin is, of course, and I'm supposed to be good at it."

"You mean," Graham limped along after her, "that Greek lessons could be arranged for you – as an extra?"

Dolly smiled at him. "I'd hate to impose."

"No imposition – of course you may learn Greek."

"You're awfully kind to me. There's just a chance I might get to university."

"Why, that would be splendid, Dolly . . . wouldn't it, Clare?"

Clare nodded mutely. So Zanny had killed again. Why couldn't the young be dropped from the nest at the fledgling stage? Why couldn't responsibility be for ever shed? Turn her in. Cut off the blood money to Dolly. (Machiavellian Dolly – why didn't we know you had Machiavellian tendencies, Dolly?) Why do Graham and I have to be so caring – so good – so burdened? Why do we have to keep on pretending?

She opened her bag and took out two small bottles of vitamin tablets. Well, she'd brought them – she might as well get rid of them. "Good for your teeth," she said.

*

92

Murphy couldn't get the smell of the mortuary out of his nose. It was over three days now since he had made the identification and he could still taste the place. It was on his palate, in his sinuses – everywhere. Bridget hadn't looked like Bridget, but of course it was. He had never seen her in repose. In death she had looked almost smug. "Yaboo, you can't reach me now," she seemed to say. "I loved you just a bit," she seemed to say. "Remember the gorse prickles?" He had nearly snapped at her to open her goddamn eyes. To let him see the smile behind them. The mortuary attendant, or someone, had draped something over her forehead where the gash was. There was supposed to be a wound on the back of her neck, too, but that couldn't be seen because she was lying on it. When he had nodded and made the identification, Mother Benedicta had come in to make everything doubly sure. The old biddy had stood stock still by the bier – or whatever it was called – taken one peek, and then taken out her rosary. Her face was as bloodless as Bridget's – two arctic masks – one beautiful, one not. While she was saying her prayers he had walked down to the other end of the room. Bridget's feet were poking out from the end of the sheet. Pretty little feet. Very clean. Very cold. Varnish on the nails, chipped a bit. He had held her feet in his hands, warming them. Mother Benedicta had come alive like Lucifer falling out of heaven and snarled at him not to touch. He had given Bridget's feet a last reassuring little squeeze and then moved back. Goodbye, Bridget. I don't believe it, but it's true.

The policeman had driven Mother Benedicta back to the convent.

He had gone on a bender.

He had been on a bender every day since it happened, but he could still smell the mortuary through the whisky fumes – so keep drinking boyo – drink – drink – drink.

"You can't go and see him," Dolly said. "If you do and you're caught, you'll be chucked out."

"And you – also," Zanny said. Being expelled didn't bother her. It would be awkward and a nuisance. The only tragic thing about being expelled would be the fact that she would no longer see Murphy. She would be sent to another school, perhaps miles away. It was essential, therefore, that she should call on him without anyone finding out. In this she needed Dolly's help. Murphy would have to be visited in the dark when the nun on dormitory duty was asleep. The only safe way out of the convent was down the fire escape which was on the landing outside the dormitory and near the bathrooms. The fire escape door was bolted at night. It was an easy matter for her to unbolt it, but if it were later checked it would be bolted again and she wouldn't be able to get back in. So it was necessary for Dolly to be around to make sure that the bolt was left alone. The lavatories were adjacent to the bathrooms. An hour or so after she had gone, Dolly would take a nocturnal trip to the lavatory – in fact, several nocturnal trips – and check the door each time.

"If you don't do it," she told her, "and I get caught, you can kiss Cambridge goodbye."

After due consideration Dolly reluctantly agreed with Zanny's statement. The nuns here had a touching faith in her. They had mothered her for years. They had almost created her. She was their shining example of what could be done with a tough little slum child who had sufficient intelligence to make the polishing up process worth while. If Zanny went, the Moncriefs would make her go, too. Another school simply wouldn't take the same interest in her.

"I think," she told Zanny, "that you're crazy."

At that particular moment she hadn't Zanny's homicidal tendency in mind. Later, on reflection, she still couldn't equate Zanny's calm killing of those who got in her way with madness. She knew exactly what she was

94

doing each time. She just didn't care.

"It isn't crazy," Zanny said, "to go and tell Murphy I'm sorry about Bridget."

"Then you're going to tell him that you . . ." Dolly didn't finish it. Little Willie's death had been out in the open between them – so had Evans the Bread – but with the passing of time Dolly had learned to be more discreet. It wasn't the sort of thing you bawled out. You didn't even state it *sotto voce*. You implied it because you knew, and it was necessary that Zanny should know you had her over a barrel. At the same time you had to be careful that you didn't find yourself inside the barrel, going downhill fast.

So you played along – carefully.

"I mean," Zanny said coldly and distinctly, "that I'm sorry that somehow Bridget fell over the cliff and died. I am going to pay my condolences."

It sounded like the rent. For cool effrontery, Dolly thought, it took the biscuit. She could imagine it very clearly. "I'm so sorry that I disposed of Bridget, Mr. Murphy. But here I am – have me instead."

"You don't pay your condolences," she told Zanny, "at eleven o'clock at night – or even later. He'll think you're going for one thing only."

Zanny thought he probably would, too, but he would be very much a gentleman about it all. She began to play the scene in her mind.

"My dear young lady," he would say when he opened the door. "My dear Zanny! How extraordinarily nice it is to see you. What a wonderful surprise . . . but why so late?"

She would then explain about the amusingly suspicious attitude of the nuns and he would laugh with her and ask her in. "A breed apart," he would say, "these religious ladies – *les religeueses*," (his French would be a great deal better than hers), "like ladies in aspic, wouldn't you say? Glued up with convention. Stuck fast in moral torpor." (Oh, he was clever, Murphy.)

He would ask her in and make her a particularly good cup of coffee. They would sit at either side of the small fireplace and he would gaze into the flames looking sad. She would then touch his hand gently and express her sympathy.

"Ah, Bridget," he would say, "a wild girl, Bridget. Wanton. Demanding. An enormous sexual appetite." He would look at her sideways then. "My little Zanny – I shock you?"

She would assure him that he did not.

The main thing was that he didn't mind much that Bridget was dead. He would be too nice to say so, of course. It would just be implied.

After that . . . well, after that . . .

Dolly cut across her thoughts. "There's supposed to be a safe time of the month, but I can't remember when it is – and there's something called interrupted coit . . . something or other – which means you stop just before it happens. For God's sake be careful."

Zanny didn't know what she was talking about.

"If you get yourself bloody pregnant," Dolly said, recognising the need for plain-speaking, "you'll be out on your ear-hole – and so will I."

"In times of stress," Zanny said, "you're downright common!"

And then – as they sometimes did – they felt a rare moment of affinity and began to giggle.

By eleven o'clock it had begun to rain; a fine thin drizzle falling from a pale grey sky. Zanny, buttoned into her mack which she had smuggled up to the dormitory, picked her way quietly and cautiously across the lawns. The nuns went to bed early and rose at six. There was a light in Miss Sheldon-Smythe's window, she was probably talking to her budgerigars, and that was the only light in the building. Poor Miss Sheldon-Smythe, Zanny thought, poor ancient, barmy, budgerigar-loving Miss Sheldon-Smythe. Fancy spending the last of your days in a place like this. Poor manless, withered, end of the road, cutter up of worms, Miss Sheldon-Smythe. My road, thought Zanny, picking her way carefully through the blackcurrant bushes bordering the path to Murphy's door, is like the Milky Way, blazing with stars.

But it was cold. Wet. More than a little muddy. Hens in their sleep sounded like babies having nightmares. Babies? Coit . . . what? Her heart was beginning to thump.

Murphy, deep in his own whisky-induced nightmare, heard the knocking on the door as nails being knocked into his skull. He was being held in an attitude of crucifixion against a huge cellar door. His hands and feet were already impaled and now they were impaling his head. The bottom of the cellar steps was awash in a pool of beer and the level of the pool was rising slowly. It gave off fumes, visible like mist on an Irish bog. That beer should give off whisky fumes was a puzzle that he found hard to solve. He moved his head slightly on the pillow and moaned with pain. If only the bastard would stop hammering. "Bloody scarper, bloody soddin' punk," he muttered.

Zanny, discovering at that point that the door was unlocked, opened it and went in. The kitchen was very dark and it took her a while to find the switch.

The light streamed out from the kitchen and into the bedroom like molten metal. And now the sods were trying to burn him. Murphy rolled about on the bed and twitched.

Zanny, in the past, had seen her father mildly inebriated. It showed in the eyes and ever so slightly in the speech. Graham, intoxicated, was exceedingly dignified. He walked with a slow, careful grace. He smelled slightly and rather sweetly.

Murphy asprawl under tumbled sheets was something quite different. His forehead was pallid with sweat. He threshed around. He smelt as if gallons of cough mixture had been spilt and mixed with kerosene.

97

He was, Zanny thought, quite obviously ill. She fought down her own sudden nausea and breathed deeply into her handkerchief. She had seen a film once in which a woman missionary looked after a hobo in a jungle hut – the hobo had something awful like cholera – but the missionary had sat beside his bed wiping away the sweat. Later in the film, when he was better, she had taken off her glasses and most of her clothes and let down her hair. And the hobo had a shave and stopped being delirious and began speaking very nicely. He had been a diplomat, or something. They had made love on a clean bit of beach outside the dirty hut and the moon had been big as a melon.

This, too, was a very dirty hut.

The wallpaper had a damp line running along the skirting board. No wonder he had pneumonia . . . or something.

He had a very beautiful body. She gazed upon it with fascination.

It was at that point that Murphy opened his eyes. An angel-whore with hair like spun gold was standing ankle deep in the whisky. The angel-whore was blushing. He pulled the shroud around him in a moment of modesty.

"Jesus, Mary and Joseph," he said.

"It's quite all right," Zanny assured him politely, "I didn't mind a bit."

There was a chair near the dressing-table with Murphy's clothes on it. Zanny put the clothes in a pile on the dressing-table and took the chair over to the bed. "I'm so sorry," she said, "to find you ill."

Murphy, losing the drift, just heard a swish of words. Purgatory was cold and wet like the inside of a beer barrel when you had drunk your fill and were awash up to your eyeballs.

"Would you," asked a voice that might have come from heaven or from hell, "like a little warm milk?"

Definitely from hell.

Milk! It might be good to vomit. So far he had resisted it.

Zanny, interpreting his silence as yes, went to look for some. She found his butter ration in a cheese dish on the draining board. In the cupboard to the right of the window was a loaf of bread, fairly fresh. Margarine. A couple of small lamb chops. Eggs in a bowl. Milk. She didn't need to sniff the milk to know it was off.

The missionary hadn't fed the hobo. She had mopped his brow. It might be better just to rinse out a cloth in warm water and do the same.

Oh, Murphy, Murphy, what a blessing I came to you, Murphy. In the days to come we'll remember this night. You – ill, sweating and smelly. I – caring for you – encouraging you through the crisis – pneumonia had a crisis, hadn't it? Not being disgusted. Not the smallest, slightest bit *put off*. Was the missionary put off? She was not. For better or for worse, Murphy. This is worse than worse, but it can't last. Anyway, the place hasn't a bathroom. Fancy the nuns putting him in a sordid dump like this. A man of his sensitivity – brought low. What was Mother Benedicta thinking of?

He wasn't just terribly drunk, was he?

No, of course not. You weaved around when you were drunk. Or were too steady like Daddy. He might have tried to dose himself with something and had too much. His stomach probably needed rest – like hers had, after the picnic. He had seen her vomit. She had burned with shame that he should have seen. Seeing him as he was now evened things up a bit. What to use for a cloth to put on his head? There was a drying-up cloth near the sink and it was clean – well, fairly. She rinsed it under the tap.

My blood is running into my eyes, Murphy thought in sudden panic as he became aware of something wet on his forehead. He shot up in bed and began threshing out with his arms. Zanny, caught across the chest, gave a little grunt of pain and moved away hastily.

Murphy, his eyes wide open, informed her calmly

that the last time blood had been taken from him it had been taken from his arm. He couldn't remember why.

Having delivered this statement, he fell flat on his back again, and descended through a night sky, crackling with purple clouds, and flashed here and there with lightning.

Zanny, abandoning the cloth as being too dangerous, drew the chair a little away from the bed and sat again, watching him cautiously. People in delirium did strange things. What had he been talking about? What, for goodness sake, should she do?

Had the decision been left to Sergeant Thomas he wouldn't have arrested Murphy at twenty minutes to midnight. A good night's sleep followed by a substantial breakfast were, he believed, comforting shock absorbers. And even for the toughest it was one hell of a shock. Detective Inspector Warrilow, however, possessed an English streak of hardness like steel in an old-fashioned corset. Since his arrival a few months ago backbones had stiffened to wary attention. The men didn't even have the satisfaction of swearing at him in Welsh. He could speak it. A fact he had kept treacherously to himself for quite a long time. Thomas, prepared to be charitable, had suggested that perhaps his motive for a night arrest was to spare the nuns the embarrassment of seeing Murphy removed. He didn't give a tinker's cuss for the nuns' embarrassment, he had replied. When wrenched roughly out of sleep, the brain was not alert. Confessions, guarded by day, tumbled out into the night air. Three a.m. was probably the best time, but he had some regard for the well-being of his men.

But regard for Murphy? What sort of joke was that supposed to be? He hadn't had any regard for Bridget O'Hare when he'd thumped her over the head and flung her over a cliff. The blood test had shown that the child she was carrying wasn't his. Had it been, he would probably have preserved the two of them. Being a

Catholic. Witnesses had heard them quarrel before they went up on the cliff. The word bastard had been used. He had returned from the cliff alone. He had pretended he had seen her. What more proof did anyone want? A confession? Well – go get the man. Batter the door down. Frighten the living daylights out of him. Play rough, boys, play rough.

It wasn't in Thomas' nature to play rough, but he had to do as he was told, within reason. He took P.C. Stevie Williams with him. Williams captained the local rugger team and looked a bit of an ape. One look at Williams and you suddenly didn't want to argue.

Zanny, awakened from a light doze by the sharp rapping on the door, felt her stomach shoot up into her throat. Somebody had split on her! Dolly had told Mother Benedicta. No, not Dolly. Somebody. God! Who? Her fingers had somehow got entwined in Murphy's. In a panic she pulled her hand free.

Mother Benedicta was bursting down the door. She was kicking it. Thumping it. Murphy was still asleep. She wanted him to fling himself in front of her. Protect her. He was snoring gently. Mother Benedicta had gone mad. She was crashing around like a raving lunatic. Get under the bed, for God's sake – quick!

Zanny disappeared just as Thomas and Williams discovered that all they had to do was raise the latch. Well, they'd been told to make a noise. They'd made it.

Zanny was aware of two pairs of feet in boots. They were marauders come to kill. Not Mother Benedicta. Oh, Mother Benedicta, better you! And then one of them spoke quite gently, his accent soft and Welsh.

"Boy bach," he said, "oh, boy bach, a skinful you've had. Light a match and the place will explode."

"A hair of the tail of the dog," the other one said, "to get him on his feet."

"Soaked right up," the first one replied, "a drop more and it will come out through his ears."

They had spoken in Welsh then, debating on how to

101

rouse Murphy enough to make him stand. A gentle rolling about on the bed caused the feather mattress to sag. Zanny felt it a couple of inches above her head. The springs of the bed were rotten. One scraped her hair. There was dust under the bed and a spider's web in the corner. She closed her eyes and prayed. "Hail Mary, full of grace . . . Holy Mary, Mother of God."

The bed was swinging like a ship at sea.

Naked feet between two pairs of boots at the bedside. Murphy's voice: "Would you hold the room steady a bit! Would you apply the bloody brakes! Would you bloody lay off!"

Thomas, very soothing. "Got to get you dressed, boy bach. Off on a little trip – see."

Murphy, disliking the idea of a little trip, attempted to get back into bed. Williams stopped him. Anybody gripped by Williams couldn't move. Thomas dressed Murphy sketchily, the best he could.

"Better say it then," said Williams, "while I hold him."

"Seems a waste of time," Thomas replied. Nevertheless he said what had to be said. He gabbled it rather fast and Zanny had to strain to hear. It wasn't until that moment that she realised that the two men were police officers and that they had come to arrest Murphy on a charge of suspicion of murdering Bridget O'Hare.

Murphy heard the charge with equanimity. He was leaning up against the bedroom door, held there by Williams' arm. He felt slightly better standing up as if the fluid were circulating in all directions and not gathered like a reservoir in his stomach and in his head. He began softly to sing about the Mountains of Mourne.

The two Welsh policemen eased him gently in the direction of the door.

The last words Zanny heard were Thomas'. "The Mountains of Mourne sweep down to the sea," he joined in with a rich deep bass. "Oh, boy bach, boy bach, sing while you can, boyo, sing while you can."

Four

When Zanny returned to the convent, bedraggled, dirty and deeply distressed, Dolly thought she had been raped. Which would have served her right. The middle classes were extraordinarily dim. Although she had been catapulted amongst them and was taking her place there with some ease, Dolly still had a firm grasp on life's realities. She knew what human nature was all about. Murphy was a male animal and a dainty morsel had been presented to him. He had devoured her in one gulp – on the floor by the looks of things. She pushed Zanny into the nearest bathroom and closed the door quietly behind them.

"Well," she hissed, "what happened?"

Zanny began to cry. Genuine, low, moaning tears. It was difficult to cry quietly. She wanted to sit on the side of the bath and howl.

Murphy . . . Murphy . . . Murphy . . . Oh, Murphy . . . Murphy . . . Murphy . . . They've taken you when they should have taken me . . . What am I going to do?

"Take your filthy mack off," Dolly said, and helped her to do just that. "And if you can't shut up, then push your head into it." It was fortunate that Sister Clemence wasn't on dormitory duty. Her hearing was as sharp as her tongue.

It took some while for Zanny to tell Dolly what had happened. Dolly received the news in silence. She was shaken. Not unduly surprised, though. One of her uncles had been put away once for a burglary he hadn't committed. He hadn't stolen a thing in his life, he had commented bitterly, just been landed with the stuff.

103

Planted had been his word. The police hadn't believed him.

Zanny's predicament, as Dolly saw it, was less moral than practical. Murphy might have an alibi, in which case he would be let off. If he hadn't, he might talk his way out of it. All Murphy had to do was to speak sweet reason to the police. The Irish were supposed to be golden-tongued, weren't they? Blarney kissed and persuasive. The uncle she barely remembered had dropped his words like clods of earth and looked as if he needed to be swept up with a brush and pan. He hadn't stood a chance. Murphy's rating was rather better – though not much. Now, if Zanny's father had been accused of pushing Zanny's mother over a cliff he would have raised an eyebrow in polite astonishment. "Good Lord, Inspector," he would have drawled, "this is really too funny for comment. My dear fellow, you're not serious?" Abject apologies would have followed.

Dolly came out of her reverie to hear Zanny's tear-choked question. "What am I going to *do*?"

"Nothing," she said. "Wait. Shut up. Do nothing."

Zanny, not too shattered to follow Dolly's self-motivated reasoning, had a vision of university towers and mortar boards. "There are such things as honour and a conscience," she said bitterly, "and not letting people suffer. But you wouldn't know anything about that."

"Honour and a conscience," Dolly said blandly, "you have to be able to afford. As for suffering – do you suppose Bridget O'Hare landed on a mattress?"

Neither knew how to break the ensuing silence.

It was necessary to go to bed.

They went.

Of all the teaching staff at the convent Miss Sheldon-Smythe took the news about Murphy with the greatest show of indignation. The day the news broke she stormed over to Mother Benedicta's study and rapped

104

on the door. "This," she said, entering without invitation and waving the newspaper, "is absolutely absurd. Ignatius Murphy is one of the kindest, most controlled men I know."

Accustomed to being laughed at – politely, of course, and not overtly – control for Miss Sheldon-Smythe was synonymous with being taken seriously. Murphy hadn't found her amusing at all. He had had a pet ferret once, he had told her, and he had liked it as much as she liked her budgerigars. Sure, it was no trouble to dig up groundsel for them – and there were apples to spare on the convent trees, no call to go buying any. A bit of apple – a bit of groundsel – and something hard to sharpen the beaks on – and she'd have the best pair of birds in all of Wales, sure she would. As for the way Miss Sheldon-Smythe chose to dress when the Royals had occasion to celebrate, that was up to her. He never raised an eyebrow at the red, white and blue waistcoat, and when she had tentatively invited comment he had said something about the Irish wearing of the green. A song, he had explained kindly.

Now, confronting Mother Benedicta, Miss Sheldon-Smythe was in deepest black. As a sartorial protest it was effective. Mother Benedicta's gloom deepened. She had no firm opinion on Murphy's guilt or innocence. He was being committed for trial and was being held in custody. The police must think they had a case. They had allowed her to see him.

Embarrassment on both sides had been almost palpable. Murphy, now quite sober, had been brought to the interview room by Sergeant Thomas. Inspector Warrilow, (though Mother Benedicta hadn't known this), had told Thomas to get rid of the nun – Mother Superior, whatever she was – as fast as he could without antagonising her. There were no grounds for objecting to the interview. "Just see it's brief."

Murphy, still numb with shock, hadn't yet warmed up into indignation. Mother Benedicta, also numb with shock, found it extraordinarily difficult to talk to him. Sergeant Thomas, not in the slightest degree shocked, wished one of his minions could have taken over. He just happened to be the only one who knew Mother Benedicta – and knowing her in this context wasn't an advantage. He had to resist a desire to offer everyone tea.

Mother Benedicta had at last asked the accused if he needed anything from the cottage. Such as his pyjamas?

Murphy, unnerved to be talking about pyjamas with Mother Benedicta, had shaken his head. He wondered if he should explain that he didn't wear them and then decided he shouldn't. This conversation wasn't at all proper. It was much easier to say that he hadn't pushed Bridget over the cliff than it was to say that he went to bed naked. He had accordingly protested his innocence.

Mother Benedicta said that she would pray for him. A non-committal response – as she had meant it to be – and that had been that.

Miss Sheldon-Smythe was by contrast passionately biased. "A very gentle man," she reiterated, sitting down. "He was unfortunate enough to be tempted by a bad girl. You knew, of course, that she was pregnant?"

Mother Benedicta hadn't known. The foetus was three months, according to the pathologist, but as yet its existence – its short-lived existence – wasn't common knowledge. The fact that according to blood tests Murphy couldn't have been the father was known only to Murphy and the police. The papers would have a field day when evidence was submitted at the trial; for the time being nobody not directly concerned wth the case knew anything about it – except, apparently, Miss Sheldon-Smythe.

Mother Benedicta digested the information before speaking, though nothing could shock her any more. "It takes two," she said succinctly. "The blame is equal." Curiosity overcame her distaste for the subject. "How did you know?"

"She told me."

If the wicked and immoral young decided to have babies out of wedlock, Mother Benedicta thought, they would hardly make a confidante of an elderly spinster who was quite obviously lacking in common sense. They would go elsewhere for comfort and advice.

"Why did she tell you?"

Miss Sheldon-Smythe's rather yellowish face became less jaundiced as she blushed. "She wanted an abortion."

Mother Benedicta felt a sudden sharp pain in her chest brought about by a vision of something quite horrific. Here at last was something she couldn't cope with. For once unable to speak, she just looked at the other woman, appalled.

"I mean," Miss Sheldon-Smythe went on hastily, aware that the wrong impression might have been given, "she needed money to pay for the abortion. She happened to know that I had recently acquired fifty pounds through an insurance policy."

Mother Benedicta began to breathe more normally, but she still couldn't speak.

"I refused to give it," Miss Sheldon-Smythe said. "A bad action shouldn't be followed by a worse one. Apart from that," she added, "at my age you don't throw money around."

"Quite," Mother Benedicta agreed faintly.

She wondered if the police knew about Bridget's baby. They probably did. She wondered if Bridget had confessed it to Father Donovan. She probably hadn't. Either way, Father Donovan couldn't be pumped on the matter. It was rather extraordinary that Murphy should have murdered the mother of his child – if he had. Dear God, she prayed silently, forgive me for employing Murphy in the first place – and for employing Bridget in the second.

Miss Sheldon-Smythe had been the only girl in a family of five boys, and had tended them with devotion.

If they drank too much or womanised too much she reproved them gently about their peccadilloes but never censured them. When, one by one, they grew up and left home, she felt her world diminish. She would have liked to have married and had sons. She would have spoiled them dreadfully. To her Murphy was a brother, a son. In this barren wilderness of a convent he had been a reminder of days gone by and days that had never arrived.

He was Murphy. He could do no wrong. He liked her budgerigars. He was kind.

"He didn't do it," she said, "he just did *not* do it. What's the matter with the judicial system in this country? Are the police maniacs?"

She went on in similar vein for some time and Mother Benedicta heard her out patiently.

"The police," she said, interrupting her at last, "probably know what they're about. I've always found Sergeant Thomas to be a man of considerable common sense. If Murphy is innocent he has nothing to fear."

"But he shouldn't be under suspicion at all. His innocence shouldn't be questioned. Haven't you felt his aura?"

"His *what?*"

"His essence – his emanations – his essential goodness." Miss Sheldon-Smythe was fingering the buttons on her black cardigan as if she wanted to pull them off one by one.

Mother Benedicta had had enough. The convent would be in a ferment of hysteria if this stupid elderly woman couldn't control herself better. "I forbid you," she said, "to speak about Murphy to the girls. If they speak about him to you, stop them. If you can't conduct your classes without reference to the garden, then don't conduct them at all. We have innocent young girls here under our care. I am relying on you to see that they are in no way disturbed or harassed by a particularly nasty situation. How old are you, Miss Sheldon-Smythe?"

The threat was implicit in the question.

"Fifty-eight," said Miss Sheldon-Smythe, who was sixty-two.

"Then you have two remaining years of good solid work – of being a good calming influence. I can rely on you in this crisis, I hope?"

Miss Sheldon-Smythe said she could. But her fires weren't quenched; they were just turned inwards for a while.

"All the same . . ." she began, her eyes smouldering.

"Pray for him," Mother Benedicta said brusquely, "and leave the rest to God."

The girls took it in turns to steal one daily newspaper from the pile in the hall until the thefts were reported by the lay staff and all newspapers banned. That their one and only beautiful male was on a murder charge angered them deeply. That he was called Ignatius, shortened by some of the cheaper newspapers to Iggy, occasioned a few giggles, but not many. This was life in the raw. Life in the future. Love. Passion. A few mourned for Bridget, but mostly they were on Murphy's side. If he had pushed her over, she had asked for it. On the whole they were rather enjoying themselves. The younger ones who were perceptive enough to sense the ban on garden topics – and the reason for it – plagued Miss Sheldon-Smythe with talk of worms and crop rotation. When she tried human biology they spoke of the heart. The skeletal system led to thoughts on a broken skull. She would have found it insupportable if they hadn't made their allegiance to Murphy so clear.

For Zanny there was no amusement in any of it.

She wished she could go home and tell her parents. (On the whole, better not.) She wondered if they had read about Murphy being committed for trial. Iggy? That was ridiculous. Ignatius – well, better than the diminutive. What had his parents been thinking of? She had looked up the meaning of the name and discovered that it was Latin for fiery. That made it rather better. His parents had chosen a Latin name. They were educated people. And he was fiery – in a nice kind of way. She imagined his parents meeting her parents. At a London hotel. His parents would be quite elderly. Their anger at the unjust accusation would be controlled. The case, of course, would be dismissed. Everyone would be careful not to say too~much about it. They would drink a toast to the future. Her future and Murphy's future. There would be approval all round. Later she and Murphy would slip away. The hotel staircase would be carpeted in red. They would go up it hand in hand. At the top they would turn and look down at the two sets of parents. Daddy would raise his wine glass in a little gesture of amusement. All would be well.

Graham, raising his whisky glass about the time that Zanny was thinking about him, drank deeply. His hand shook. "Jesus Christ!" he said.

Clare folded and re-folded the newspaper as if diminishing its bulk also diminished its impact. She wasn't a praying woman, but wished she were. Suffer little children, she thought, to come unto Me. At that moment she wished Zanny were dead. It was a terrible wish and had to be squeezed out of her mind like a dark stain. You loved your children no matter what – didn't you? All right – you tolerated them, no matter what. You put up with them. You suffered them. You agonised over them.

What the hell were they going to do about Murphy?

Now that they had seen his photograph in the newspaper Zanny's motive for murder was perfectly clear. He was a desirable male. Very attractive. She had coveted him. As she had coveted Monkey of long ago – but differently. And got rid of the opposition.

"We could," Graham suggested, "see that he gets a reasonable defending barrister."

Clare looked at him pityingly. He was at times extremely naïve. She explained why they couldn't – on two counts. The first – they couldn't afford it. The second – it would implicate Zanny.

"Why should we," she asked, "pay for the defence of a man we don't know?"

"Because we are under a moral obligation."

"To shop our daughter – that's what it would amount to."

To shop or not to shop, that was the question. Both knew the answer.

"Let's hope," Clare said, "that she doesn't tell us. As yet we don't know – officially."

"Dolly told us."

"Damn Dolly!"

Graham agreed. "As far as I can see," he said with some hope, "the prosecution won't have much to go on. Had he been charged with strangling her or shooting her the case against him would be bleak. Pushing her over the cliff takes some proving."

Murphy was to be tried at the Assize Court in the early autumn. They decided to let Zanny go and spend the summer holidays with a pen-friend in Caen in Normandy. The less they saw of her at this sensitive time the better. Zanny's tongue, crippled by a foreign language, wasn't likely to do any damage there.

They would, of course, go to the trial. It would be like being pressed firmly down onto a bed of nails. A self-imposed martyrdom. Life, these days, wasn't comforting.

But it was nothing to the martyrdom of Murphy. Being held on remand to await trial for a crime he hadn't committed was a shock. He had never been inside a prison before. The poaching he had done in his youth had been skilful enough to evade capture. Not that the local farmers of Kerry would have prosecuted – a few rounds of small-shot up the backside was about their measure.

111

During the long slow weeks of the pre-trial period he had endured everything as best he could. Bridget's being three months pregnant had astonished him. At first, when his solicitor told him, he hadn't believed it. Later, alone in his cell, his anger had grown and he had thumped the wall. What sod had had Bridget before he had her? Damn it, he might have married her. Would she have told him? Or lied about the date? Women were rare schemers. The constable on duty, hearing the thumps, had come into his cell to calm him and they'd had a heart-to-heart. "Women, boy bach," he told Murphy, "are the death of many a fine fellow." It had been a kindly and earnest comment, well meant, but not tactful.

And now the time of waiting was over and he was sitting here in this great room that looked like a nonconformist chapel. Up in the pulpit was a judge who was to be called M'Lud. His wig looked as if it had been shorn from an ancient Kerry sheep, and under it, his face, long and lean, was as joyless as a Protestant sabbath. "Not a bad bloke," Prester, his defending counsel, had told him, "if you handle him properly . . . or rather, if *I* handle him properly, which I will. Catesby, for the Crown, is a bit of a pain. Remember not to lose your cool. Be polite." "Yes, sorr," said Murphy. It seemed to him that he had been exceedingly polite to a lot of people who hadn't deserved it for a long time. The end, however, was in sight. Today they had given him his best serge suit to wear. Respectable for when he went home.

The public has certainly turned out for him – the court was packed. He imagined them in the one and nine-pennies at the local cinema. "Murphy the Murderer" by Metro Goldwyn Mayer. Roar, lion, roar. It was all so daft he couldn't believe it.

He noticed Father Donovan's bald head and was pleased he was there. The old man had visited him frequently in the local gaol and they had talked a lot tribution before the fun commences." He handed over what he privately thought of as penance money and Mother Benedicta accepted the cheque with a few suitable words of appreciation.

At this stage, she told the assembled audience, some of the senior girls would entertain everyone with an outdoor ballet.

The Greek dance was the sole contribution of Robina Blane who was now counting her days until the end of the autumn term and her escape from teaching for ever. The long, salaried summer holiday had been the bait that had hooked her into this second term. It hadn't been worth it. The death of Bridget and the impending execution of Murphy would forever colour her time in this terrible place with tones of deepest gloom. Her personality, never very strong, had faded even more during the last weeks. She was a poor teacher. She didn't like the girls much. But she could dance, and so – given encouragement – could they. Three violins and a cello formed background music as they trooped onto the square of lawn directly in front of Sir Clifford, his wife, and Mother Benedicta.

Their legs, Sir Clifford thought, were pretty good. And the little white Greek outfits, though not very revealing, at least showed areas of thigh. The pubescent female could be an exciting creature. Looking around he had noticed one or two rather more than presentable examples. The girls – some had pretty good bosoms, too – raised their arms, pointed their toes, and began to dance. They weren't bad. On the whole, it wasn't such a bad place to be. It would be better if he could take a surreptitious drink of whisky. That might be possible later on.

The first dance, rather quiet and slow, lulled the mood of everyone watching it. Some of the audience settled themselves on the grass. Bees hummed. The violins were punctuated occasionally by a cheep from an interested bird.

together. He had told the priest about meeting Bridget on the cliffs and been honest about everything they'd done – well, maybe not quite everything. If the old boy thought making love was a kiss and a cuddle, that was up to him. He didn't know if his hesitancy about personal physical details had been misconstrued by Father Donovan but to his direct: "Did you kill her?" his emphatic "No!" had seemed to be accepted. All the same, at his most recent confession the old man had been like a carpenter with a screwdriver trying to dislodge a rusty nail. "The Lord is compassionate," he had said, "don't be afraid to tell me the truth."

Murphy wasn't afraid to tell it. But, as he was to discover during the two days of the trial, truth was a peculiar commodity. Pliable and capable of distortion. A lot was made of a little, and important truths ignored. Forensic experts went to a great deal of trouble to prove that he and Bridget had been together on that precise area of headland. Their scientific evidence concerned soil and seeds and fibres from their clothes. All they had to do, Murphy thought, was ask. He had never denied being there. And he wouldn't deny they'd made love – so why employ a scientist to discover that? The way the scientist described it, it didn't sound like love – more like a clinical operation. Catesby, the prosecuting counsel, even had the cheek to suggest it was "an angry taking of a woman after a violent row". As for Bridget's passionate scratches, he called those, "a desperate woman's attempt to get away". While listening to all this rubbish Murphy began to understand why the prison doctor had taken such an interest in the nail marks on his shoulder. The true explanation was simple enough. Embarrassing, perhaps, but necessary.

When he was called to the witness box on the second day he made sure that he swore on the Douai version of the New Testament. It didn't do to take chances. This was important.

He stated his case immediately. He and Bridget had

113

been on the headland making love. The scratches were part of love. "No violence, sorr, at all."

Catesby stopped him abruptly. Murphy was there to answer questions, he told him, and be silent until they were asked. Then, after a brief re-capping of events, he lunged in for the attack. "You have heard the evidence given by the two witnesses who were sitting on the beach as you and Bridget O'Hare passed by them on the way up to the promontory. You were, they say, quarrelling with some passion. The word bastard was used with great bitterness. I put it to you that you had discovered her infidelity with another man and that she had told you about the child she was expecting."

"No," said Murphy.

"You didn't know about the child?"

"No."

"Oh, come, come, you're not going to tell me you weren't quarrelling?"

"We were quarrelling, sorr," Murphy said, "about a bastard."

"The young woman's child – you mean?"

"No child is a bastard," Murphy said, quoting Father Donovan. "Every child is a child of God."

The sentiment, though commendable, didn't clarify anything, and Murphy's remark was followed by a brief silence.

"Perhaps," Catesby suggested silkily, "you can explain?"

"We were quarrelling," Murphy said, "about Charlie Parnell."

"And Charlie Parnell," ventured Catesby, "is the bastard who had relations with your girlfriend, Bridget O'Hare? He is, then, the father of her unborn child?"

"'Twould be a miracle," Murphy said, astonished by the notion. "An immaculate conception."

Prester jumped up. "If your Lordship pleases . . ." He had warned Murphy not to get on to this. The thick Irishman would do well to keep his politics under lock

114

and key. Only another Irishman could hope to understand them. "The defendant," he explained, "is referring to Charles Stewart Parnell, the Irish Nationalist leader. He died in 1891."

There was a titter around the court.

The judge frowned. His was an ancient and esteemed office, he wasn't presiding over a music hall. He wished Catesby would conduct his case more expertly and avoid this sort of deplorable irrelevance. "You would be wise to behave with more gravity," he warned Murphy. "You are facing a serious charge."

He nodded at Catesby to proceed.

"Are you seriously telling me," Catesby asked, annoyed at having been made to look a fool, "that you and Bridget O'Hare were quarrelling about Irish politics?"

"Yes, sorr."

"You were out together on a nice sunny day – having a picnic – she was your girlfriend – your lover – she was pregnant with another man's child – and you quarrelled about a man who lived in the last century?"

"Yes, sorr."

"I find it," Catesby said, "quite incredible."

He continued to express his scepticism, and to suggest more likely motives for murder, before finally sitting down.

Prester, the defending counsel, took the floor. It was difficult to make the incredible believable, but he tried. "After several conversations with the defendant," he said, "I am now rather more knowledgeable about the Irish troubles – and the Irish temperament – than I was before. It is natural for the Irish to take sides – especially over their own national heroes. A hero to Bridget. A bastard to Murphy. An argument of some considerable heat at the time – but short lived. Murphy did not push Bridget over the cliff because she put up an impassioned defence of Charles Stewart Parnell. He did not push her over the cliff at all."

He then went on to try and prove it. The situation was so negative in many ways that proof either way was very difficult to establish. The pathologist's report about a blow over the back of the head wasn't helpful. She had been found face downwards in the gully. The sea might have rolled stones across the back of her head and rolled them off again, but the nature of the wound was consistent with one hard thump. Had the murder instrument been an old tin of – say, corned beef weighted with pebbles – the lacerations of the skin would have cried murder in tones loud and clear. As it was, she had probably been hit pretty hard by a stone – Prester did his best with stones being dislodged as she fell and falling on her. But it was weak and he knew it.

Had Murphy said he had left her alive – which he did say and insisted upon – and left it at that, he might have been believed. But his insistence that he had later seen her was worse than weak, it was damning. She could have fallen over the cliff – picking flowers perhaps on the slippery grass. She could have had a knock on the back of the head as she fell. It would have been natural for Murphy to go back and look for her – which he did. It would have been natural for him not to have thought of looking over the edge of the cliff. He hadn't, he said, thought of looking. But it was not natural – or credible – that he should have gone back to the cliff and then returned to the nuns in a rage and saying that he had seen her getting into a mythical boat with mythical yachtsmen. Why a boat if he didn't know she was dead in the water? Why not a car? A bus?

"Murphy," Catesby said, making the most of it in his final speech, "was a frightened man – not an angry man at this stage – a man terrified by the consequences of what he had done – the consequences of his dastardly crime. And so he pretends he saw Bridget putting out to sea. The sea would carry her into the gully. If he were lucky it would carry her out again and she would disappear for ever more, or else be washed up in several months' time too decomposed for identification. But the sea didn't carry her out. And by the way she fell it couldn't have carried her in. So there you have it, ladies and gentlemen of the jury. A corpse that refuses to budge from the site where it landed. A corpse of a beautiful young girl – a beautiful young mother-to-be. And there you have Murphy – a passionate man – a jealous man – and not only that, a devious man. It took some acting, wouldn't you say, to show anxiety to the nuns when Bridget didn't appear. It took acting to simulate anger when he returned from the search – it took cunning to state that he had seen her alive. A simple confession – a heartbroken "I pushed her, God help me" – a change of plea to guilty might have aroused compassion in you – and indeed in me. We are all fallible. All human. We err. We sin. We transgress. But we do not kill and then try to cover up the crime. Do you see a contrite man standing there? You do not. Earlier he had the audacity to joke. Is the death of a nineteen-year-old girl funny? Ladies and gentlemen, it is appalling. It is tragic. It is unforgivable."

And so he went on. For another ten minutes.

Prester in his final speech couldn't compete.

The judge had little to add at the summing up. Catesby, after a fumbling start, had pressed on the accelerator and revved up to a satisfactory finish. However, it was up to the jury. He instructed them without obvious bias, but the bias was there, sensed and powerfully persuasive.

While they were out Murphy went below and played draughts with one of the prison officers while the other one fetched him tea. To play draughts and drink tea was his way of showing willing. He was part of a charade – a short-lived, amazingly stupid charade – in which everyone behaved like lunatics. It was polite to sit here and jump his white draughts over the black ones. His opponent was letting him win. His opponent looked bloody sympathetic. When all this nonsense was over, he told

117

him, he was going back to Ireland. The auld fella, his father, was getting on a bit, he could do with help on the farm.

The jury were out for three hours.

When they came back in they didn't look at Murphy.

Murphy thought he hadn't heard their leader properly when he gave the verdict. It wasn't until he saw the judge putting the black bit of cloth on his head that he knew what was happening.

The bastards were going to hang him!

The bastards were going to bloody do him in!

For a moment he felt like picking up the two prison officers who were standing beside him and slamming them down over the side of the dock. He had a vision of garotting the judge with the bit of black on his bloody wig. Anger like a roaring sea screamed through his head.

But he stood in complete silence.

The judge asked him if he had anything to say.

He was incapable of saying anything. He was incapable of moving. After a few minutes the prison officers led him away.

"I am very much afraid," Clare said, "that I can't eat this tea-cake." It was extraordinary, she thought, how you did ordinary things in times of great disaster – such as leaving the courtroom and ordering tea in a little café adjacent to it. Even the old priest, Father Donovan, was doing it. And he was eating his tea-cake – even putting more butter on it. Shouldn't he be down in the cells holding Murphy's hand – praying over him – doing something? Shouldn't she and Graham have stood up in the court and shouted "Stop!" Couldn't they, even now, waylay the judge and tell him how abominably wrong the jury's verdict was?

Well, of course they could.

But they wouldn't.

They'd sit down at a window table with a red and

white checked cloth on it and they would order tea and toasted tea-cakes. Graham would even eat them. She looked at him in disgust.

"If you don't want yours," he said, "I'll have it," and helped himself.

Despite the awful fate that was facing Murphy, Graham felt marginally less worried about Zanny now. The case against Murphy had been strong. Circumstantial evidence, but plausible. He might even have done it; twelve intelligent jurors believed he had.

He put this to Clare. "We could have misinterpreted Dolly's insinuations. Or they could have been made through spite. We were fools to listen to her."

Clare didn't answer. The lethal events in the past, concerning Zanny, Graham had been told about but hadn't seen. He hadn't been there when Peter had lifted little Willie out of the pond and tried to revive him . . . while Zanny stood by. It was she who had been walking down that country road when Evans the Bread's van came thundering around the corner – not Graham. He hadn't felt the heartstopping shock of seeing Zanny's attempt to push Dolly under the wheels. All the information he had received had been diluted to some extent in the telling. For her, today's horror hadn't been diluted by anything anybody had had to say. Murphy was about to suffer for something Zanny had done. She was sure of it. He had stood in the witness box, bewildered, saying all the wrong things. She could have wept for him.

"God damn Zanny," she burst out in sudden fury.

Graham looked at her shocked.

Father Donovan overheard the young woman at the window table goddamning somebody and wished that the Lord's name wasn't taken so lightly. "And may the Lord have mercy on your soul," had been said in all seriousness by the judge. And may He have mercy on yours, M'Lud, Father Donovan thought with some passion. It was wrong for anybody to kill anybody, but what

119

could he, an ageing parish priest, do about it? Nothing. Murphy should not have killed Bridget – if he had. But killing *him* didn't make it any better. Old Testament justice belonged to Old Testament times. A guilty Murphy swinging on the end of a rope surely wouldn't occasion rejoicing in Heaven. And an innocent Murphy swinging should bring forth roars of celestial rage. It was a pity that the good Lord tended to be mute on such occasions. In the meantime he would have to give Murphy as much help as he could – what was it, three weeks between sentencing and execution?

And right now he would have to go back to the convent and tell Mother Benedicta to get off her knees and stop praying for an acquittal. The assault on heavenly ears would now have to broach the question of a miracle. By God, he had badly needed this good, strong cup of tea and this buttery tea-cake. The trial had left him feeling as weak as a kitten.

Mother Benedicta received the news of Murphy's sentence with icy calm. The papers, she had no doubt, would carry screaming headlines in the evening editions. Her duty, as she saw it, was to protect the girls from the trauma to the best of her ability. They would have to be told, of course, but not by the yellow press. No newspaper while the news was still hot was to be allowed anywhere near them.

She chose to tell them after Benediction in the evening. In the morning might have been better, but the convent had wireless sets and she couldn't confiscate the lot.

It was very sad and unfortunate, she said crisply, but they were not to dwell on it. When they said their rosary they could think of Bridget – and of Murphy, too – and of all the countless people who had died young – of war wounds – accidents – and other causes too numerous to mention. Her speech diluted death into little raindrops of pain in a sea of mortality. As an exercise in minimising horror it succeeded reasonably well. Some of the girls turned pale – some felt sick. But nobody actually got sick, and nobody cried. The opiate lasted for several hours.

For Zanny it began to wear off about midnight.

She had seen Bridget dead and hadn't felt a thing. She visualised Murphy facing death and couldn't bear it. Cold and shivering she crept into Dolly's bed. Dolly, unwelcoming, lay rigid.

"What can I do?" Zanny moaned, her head under the clothes, in case she was again accused of lesbianism. "What can I do?"

"If you've got a conscience – which I doubt – " Dolly said, "there's just one thing you can do – so bloody do it."

Her own conscience, very finely balanced, had come down slowly on Murphy's side. If the Moncriefs wouldn't see her through university because Zanny was languishing in gaol, then the nuns probably would – or she'd get a scholarship – or something. Academic success shouldn't depend on Murphy's broken neck. But if it did, then Murphy's neck came first. She decided that if Zanny didn't confess she'd tell Mother Benedicta anyway. It was not good policy, however, to tell Zanny this. You don't tell a keg of dynamite that you've got a box of matches handy and intend striking one – not when the keg of dynamite was right beside you.

Zanny, weeping and snuffling under the bed-clothes, wiped her nose disgustingly on Dolly's sheet. Dolly, unaware of this, gave her ten minutes to calm herself. Murphy, she thought, must have been a bit of a berk. Anybody with any sense could have talked himself out of it. He must have had a rotten defending counsel or a very biased judge. If I were his barrister, she thought, he would be back in his cottage now soaked up to his neck in whisky, not fearing for it in an abominable little cell. Her future, nebulous until now, began to take shape. There weren't many women barristers, but this was the middle of the twentieth century and time for

121

things to change. Women judges, too. She visualised herself in gown and wig holding forth in the Old Bailey. Someone like Murphy would be in the dock. A muscular hunk – brainless – innocent. The prosecuting barrister would gouge him with rapier thrusts of wit and render him speechless. The judge, uncaring about the outcome, would sit with glazed eyes. And then she, Dolly, would take centre stage. Coolly, carefully, she would demolish the case for the Crown. Murphy would stand erect with newly gained dignity. The judge would wake up and look at her with respect. The opposing barrister would bluster vainly before wilting into defeat. All her ancestors – the long line of Mortons who had never been on the winning side of anything – would send up a ghostly cheer.

Dolly Morton, K.C.

It would happen. She never dreamed. She planned. She knew now what she wanted to do. It was possible. She would do it. If this Murphy couldn't be saved, then there would be others.

If Zanny were the prisoner and she were the prosecuting counsel . . . that was more difficult. Zanny's toes touched hers. She could hear her breathing. She had known her for a long time. Lots of people had probably known Caligula for a long time . . . and Salome. On the other hand, that Scottish bloke, Robert the Bruce, wouldn't have tolerated his spider – even liked it a bit – if he hadn't been forced to live with it.

All right – then let another barrister prosecute Zanny.

Let another judge sentence her.

At least no one would hang her now – she was too young.

The ten minutes were up and she told her to push off. "I want to get some sleep."

"I," Zanny whispered in despair, "will never sleep again."

Five

That night Miss Sheldon-Smythe slept even less than Zanny. The verdict had come as no shock to her. She had lived with the possibility ever since Murphy had been taken into custody. She had also lived with a mysterious lump in her breast. It could, of course, be benign. It probably wasn't. She didn't want to know. If things were to happen, they would happen. When you were sixty-two you began to see death as a kind of cosy relationship. You lived with it as you might live with an old aunt. She was behind a closed door, undemanding, not frightening. One day you would open the door and go in to her – permanently. Now you just had the occasional chat. It was different when you were in Murphy's position. Death at his age was a vicious enemy – you fought it with everything you had – you didn't submit. And if fighting did no good then someone else lifted the sword for you.

After a lot of thought and some very careful planning, Miss Sheldon-Smythe raised her sword on Murphy's behalf the following morning.

Luckily, Mother Benedicta, unlike most Mother Superiors, was readily available to any pupil or member of staff who wished to speak to her. She was to be found in her study, if she were not busy elsewhere, between ten-thirty and eleven o'clock every morning.

On this particular morning she was standing by her study window looking at the lengthening grass of the convent lawns. It was difficult to get a replacement for Murphy. Part-time gardners didn't do such a good job. As for the hens and the rabbits, the lay sisters did the best they could with them. Those who were of farming stock could turn a living hen into a dead fowl without

123

too many qualms, but the rabbits, furry and rather beautiful, were another matter. They were breeding extremely fast; soon there wouldn't be enough hutches for them. They had been a very good idea when Murphy was around. Now, in his absence, they were not. Life was full of small problems. Small problems were therapeutic. If you filled your mind with trivia, you hadn't much space for anything else. You wished you had no space at all for Miss Sheldon-Smythe. But she was standing at the door, the newspaper in her hand. "Murphy to Hang" was the headline. "Brutal Murder by Convent Gardener" was the line under it.

"I hope," Mother Benedicta asked coldly, "that you haven't let any of the pupils see that?"

Miss Sheldon-Smythe walked across the room with some dignity and stood at Mother Benedicta's side. She didn't see the untidy grass. She saw bright sunlight on yellow roses. It was a pretty enough world. There were pretty creatures in it, such as her budgerigars. Someone, she supposed, would look after her budgerigars. They would miss her. It should be a sad thought that no one else would miss her, but it wasn't. Families with their obligations tended to thrust obstacles in the way. Property was a similar stumbling block. You owned a nice little house or a flat. You acquired things for it. You had a china cabinet full of knick-knacks – a vase you got in Greece – glass from Venice. They evoked memories. They held you – made you less free. She had sold up her house to help her youngest brother pay his gambling debts. It had seemed a big thing to do at the time – very heroic. He had been awfully grateful. If he hadn't been killed in the war he might have paid her back. All her five brothers had predeceased her . . . but they had drifted away and lost contact quite a long time before that. You got used to everything. It really didn't matter much.

"No," she said, answering Mother Benedicta's question, "nobody else has seen this. It really is quite ridiculous, of course."

And so is your mourning, Mother Benedicta thought. Why can't you wear a white collar, or something – even a chiffon scarf? "It's the will of God," she said automatically, trying to quench her uncharitable feelings. Of course Miss Sheldon-Smythe was upset. They were all upset. But it didn't do to parade your feelings.

"No, it isn't," Miss Sheldon-Smythe said calmly. "It's a gross miscarriage of justice." She watched a starling alighting on a yellow rose and then flying off again. "Murphy didn't kill Bridget O'Hare," she said. "I did."

Mother Benedicta's mind went blank for almost a minute as if a giant wave had come and washed a beach clean. All trivia – all flotsam and jetsam – disappeared. She clutched the window ledge until her legs felt strong enough and then walked from the window and over to her desk. She sat down.

"Oh?" she said.

Miss Sheldon-Smythe still stood at the window. Convents were gracious places. The staircase here was particularly beautiful. At the top of the first flight was a statue of the Virgin. A lovely little Virgin in blue and white plaster. The stairs then divided to the right and to the left and on the next landing was a statue of Saint Agnes. On each landing was a wide window – wider than this one – overlooking the gardens. All this she would miss. She wouldn't miss her room. It overlooked the courtyard at the back and had little sun. Murphy had put a couple of pots of geraniums where she could see them, but otherwise there was no colour.

"Yes," she said, almost dreamily. "I pushed her over the cliff."

Mother Benedicta had recovered her equilibrium. "No doubt," she said tartly, her anger rising, "she had annihilated your canary?" And may the Blessed Virgin forgive me, she thought, but I cannot tolerate the babbling of a lunatic at this awful time. "I beg your pardon," she said. "I had no right to be discourteous."

Miss Sheldon-Smythe, during the night hours, had prepared herself to be received with scepticism. Mother Benedicta's tongue despite her daily chanting of prayers could be vicious.

"Budgerigars," she corrected her, "two of them. And no – my reason wasn't frivolous." She sat down on a red plush chair in the window recess. There was a smear of polish on the mahogany arm; she rubbed it thoughtfully with her finger. The speech she had prepared had become fragmented in her mind. On such a lovely morning it was very difficult to talk about. She concentrated her mind on Murphy sitting in his cell. Only that way was it possible.

"You may remember," she said, "that Bridget O'Hare wanted to borrow fifty pounds from me so that she might pay for an illegal abortion. I told you that I refused her. That was a lie."

She looked up to see how Mother Benedicta was taking it. Her face was expressionless. She went on: "She was so persuasive – so upset – that in a weak moment I gave her the money. Afterwards, when I had time to think about it, I regretted it. I don't have to remind you of the Church's view on abortion. My conscience worried me. I tried to have another talk with Bridget, but here with the children around it was very difficult. On the day of the picnic I decided, on the spur of the moment, to drive over to the picnic site. There was just a possibility I might see Bridget on her own. I didn't join the picnic party and I didn't park anywhere near the school bus. For most of the time I was on the main beach. I saw Bridget and Murphy going up on to the headland and later I saw Murphy coming back on his own. That was my chance and I took it. I went up onto the headland and saw Bridget sitting on the grass. I tried having a kind and rational discussion with her, but she wouldn't listen. She called me a stupid old

126

woman and told me to stop pestering her. We were standing now – rather near the edge. She had her handbag in her hand, I thought she might have the money in it. I tried to take it from her. She backed away and lost her footing. The grass was very slippy. She fell over the edge before I could stop her. I didn't mean to kill her, but I did. Murphy had absolutely nothing to do with it at all."

"Oh, yes?" said Mother Benedicta. It was very plausible. She didn't believe a word of it. "And why didn't you tell me all this before?"

"There was always the possibility," Miss Sheldon-Smythe said, "that Murphy would be acquitted. I am not a very brave woman, Ma Mère. In fact, my silence was extremely cowardly."

If I were your mother in fact – were that physically possible – Mother Benedicta thought, I would have handed you a modicum of common sense. You are an emotional old woman, Miss Sheldon-Smythe, and what you are doing is very quixotic and makes me so cross I could scream at you. I am uncharitable. I am intolerant. I have a great many sins to confess. But this particular fantasy sin of yours makes me so angry I can't speak.

Miss Sheldon-Smythe, waiting for a moment, waited in vain. Why wouldn't she believe her? It was all perfectly feasible. Murderers had been convicted for less likely reasons.

She stood up. "I am on my way to inform the police," she said. "It seemed polite to come to you first. If I don't return, then I am being held in custody."

"I shall, of course," Mother Benedicta said rather tartly, "bear that possibility in mind."

A few minutes after Miss Sheldon-Smythe left the convent grounds in her Morris Eight, Mother Benedicta put a phone call through to the police station and asked for Sergeant Thomas. Anyone not knowing Miss Sheldon-Smythe might not immediately assess her character. It was necessary that she should be protected from her own folly. She proceeded to put it to Sergeant Thomas as delicately as she could.

After thanking her very much for telling him Thomas said that Murphy had brought his own troubles on his own head and that the law was the law and that he'd heard that the town was getting up a petition for a reprieve. They always did. It rarely worked. The verdict, though he didn't tell Mother Benedicta this, had taken almost everyone by surprise. Welsh justice usually leaned so far back from the death penalty that it almost keeled over. This time it hadn't.

Miss Sheldon-Smythe, unaware that the thorny path of martyrdom was to be carpeted over with the polite tolerance accorded to the mildly unbalanced, had packed a small suitcase and put it on the back seat. She felt extraordinarily happy as she drove along. This was one good worthwhile deed that would forever justify her existence. She didn't think they would hang her, but if they did the rope would beat the lump in her breast. If they didn't, the lump would win. Either way, Murphy, young fit and handsome, would walk free. He might even look after her budgerigars for her. She had a vivid recollection of his thick forefinger poking through the bars of the cage as he pushed the little swing.

Swing.

Oh no, Murphy, not you.

Smiling and unaware she drove past the bus-stop where Zanny and Dolly were waiting for the town bus.

"The old b.," Dolly said, "she might have given us a lift."

They were on their way to the dentist. Ostensibly. The only way to get into the town at short notice was to have a raging toothache, so Zanny, wan and distraught, had convinced Sister Agnes that she was in immediate need of an extraction. She would need to have someone with her, Sister Agnes said; she herself was too busy. Zanny, counting on this, had suggested Dolly. The older girls were allowed into the town, if the reason were good enough, in pairs, and Sister Agnes, aware of Dolly's good sense, agreed. It was a pity for Dolly to lose a morning's tuition, she said, but she could probably catch up rather quicker than most.

The dental appointment was booked over the telephone for eleven-thirty. The reason for Zanny's non-arrival would become clear in the evening newspaper. Zanny read it in her mind. "Schoolgirl on Murder Remand. Heroic Confession by Susannah Moncrief. Murphy To Go Free."

"If she had stopped," she pointed out, "she would have landed us at the dentist's – even gone in with us."

At that particular moment the removal of a tooth seemed as easy as gently pulling a daisy out of the grass. Pain was relative.

Oh, Murphy, Murphy. I love you, Murphy. One day in the future when I come out, you'll be waiting for me. "Zanny – my dearest Zanny," you'll say, "you laid down your life for me – greater love has no man – no woman . . ." Or, no – he wouldn't – that was too Biblical. He wouldn't say anything at all. He would look at her with those beautiful soft brown eyes. He would take her by the hand into the bedroom – the carpet would be white – all the furniture would be white. The only touch of colour would be a crimson nightdress on the bed. Chiffon with swirls of white lace. A negligée. Not a nightdress. It would be open all down the front. She would stand facing him, the negligée falling open. He would put his hands on her waist. On the warm, firm skin of her waist. His body – his lovely naked body – would come closer – closer . . .

"Here's the bleeding bus," said Dolly.

Dolly, when upset, kicked words around like an urchin booting an old tin can. When Zanny had asked her to accompany her she had sworn quite luridly, but couldn't refuse. It was difficult to rationalise her mood. Zanny for once in her life was doing the Right Thing.

That she would probably end up in a Borstal for doing it, she didn't seem to know. Then there would be a women's prison – years of it. Zanny's imagination was like a butterfly's wing spread delicately over a turd. Dolly, honour bound, had pointed at the turd.

Zanny's nose gently wrinkling in disapproval had said something about casting down her life that Murphy might be saved.

"It's a great pity you cast down Bridget's life in the first place," Dolly replied tartly.

It was a ten minute bus ride into the centre of the town. They weren't sure where the police station was and had to be directed. It had been Zanny's decision to by-pass Mother Benedicta and go directly to the police. She knew Mother Benedicta. She didn't know the police. Mother Benedicta, when angry, could scare the pants off you. Why be bludgeoned twice, she thought, when one confession would do? They thought they were at the wrong place when they saw Miss Sheldon-Smythe's car parked outside.

"Perhaps she's lost something," Zanny said, "and has come to complain."

"Such as what?" Dolly asked, scowling. "Her virginity?"

Dolly's ill humour was something that Zanny couldn't understand. This was her confession, not Dolly's. She needed to be bolstered up so that this, her finest hour, could be lived through with both courage and grace.

"I wish," she said crossly, "that you weren't so cross." Tears, near the surface, appeared briefly and went.

They decided to wait in the café across the road from the police station until Miss Sheldon-Smythe emerged. Zanny, who would have preferred a raspberry fizz, ordered coffee. Dolly, not geared to drama, had a raspberry fizz.

Miss Sheldon-Smythe was sipping the cup of tea that

Sergeant Thomas had provided. She had written down the statement as he had suggested and now he was reading it through.

He reminded her very much of Oswald, her middle brother, who had become an insurance broker. He had the same shock of grey hair and hadn't any lobes to his ears. He had the same way of speaking, too, rather slow, very soothing. A thick Welsh accent, of course, that was the only difference.

"Well, now, Miss Smythe – Miss Shelly-Smythe – " Thomas said, "there's just one little thing we have to get straight. In what form was the fifty pounds – ten shilling notes – pound notes – or a mixture of the two?"

"A mixture of the two," (less easy to trace?) "and it's Sheldon not Shelly – not that I mind, but you need to get it correct for the record."

Thomas apologised. Shelly. Sheldon. It made no odds. The confession would go in the loonies' file. It was funny how the publicity surrounding a capital murder case brought out the latent lunacy in people. She was a nice old body in her way – very prim and proper. A very strong motherly instinct, he guessed, badly thwarted. He had an aunt like her whose speciality was beef tea for upset stomachs and a revolting concoction of senna pods if you were bound up.

"And after you pushed her over the cliff," Sergeant Thomas said, "you took the money out of her bag?"

"Yes – as I told you. Unfortunately the wind scattered it. When you find it" (which you won't) "you'll test the notes for fingerprints – hers and mine. And I think that is all the proof you'll need. In the event of your not finding it, then I'm afraid you'll have to accept the truth as I'm telling it to you now."

"Well – now – " Thomas said, "the wind around the coast blows like the devil in pain – those notes of yours, they'll be winging their way to Ireland by now. Fond of Murphy, were you?"

"I hardly knew him." Miss Sheldon-Smythe looked

down at her bony hands in her lap. "I just don't like a miscarriage of justice, that's all. I am perfectly prepared to pay for my sin."

"Well, yes," said Thomas. Convents tended to be rather obsessed by sin. His own chapel wasn't much better. Woe is me, he thought, for I am undone and there is no good in me.

"I have brought an over-night case," Miss Sheldon-Smythe indicated a small leather suitcase by her chair, "in the event of your detaining me in your cell."

Thomas recoiled. "The cell," he said, recovering himself, "is just a little squalid." He could imagine her sitting on the rough brown blanket of the bed. She would wear a white cotton nightdress buttoned up to the neck. She would have metal curlers in her hair. Her teeth would be in one of the gaol cups. She would hang her cardigan – her black cardigan – over the peep hole in the door before getting undressed.

"Naturally," Miss Sheldon-Smythe said, "I wasn't expecting the Ritz."

"No – but – um – not very nice for a lady."

"I wasn't aware" (very frosty) "that class distinction existed in His Majesty's prisons. I am quite prepared to put up with anything that a charwoman would put up with. We are all women under the skin."

To imagine Miss Sheldon-Smythe in her skin wasn't cheering. It was time to bring the interview to an end.

"Quite," Thomas said. "Oh yes, indeed, quite. But the law is very thorough. There is a great deal to look into. Enquiries will be made. If any of those notes turn up then the forensic department will have to test them – as you said yourself. As soon as we know – beyond any doubt – then you will be placed under arrest and charged."

Miss Sheldon-Smythe felt her mouth go dry with panic. What a fool she'd been! If they were going to wait for the notes to turn up they would wait for ever. They hadn't got that long.

"As a matter of fact," she said, "I burnt the notes. I knew Bridget's prints were on them and I was afraid they would be connected with me. If you will let me write my statement again, then I'll make it quite clear. I really am so dreadfully sorry."

Sergeant Thomas was beginning to feel irritable. Diawch! but this woman was wasting his time. He suggested that Constable Williams should take over while she revised her confession.

"And then you will arrest me?"

"No," he replied with commendable calm, "but you will be arrested in time."

"Before Murphy dies?"

"Well before," he said, "oh, long, long before. Why not go along to your doctor and get something to make you better – a good tonic for the nerves – something to make you sleep?"

"I am perfectly sane," Miss Sheldon-Smythe said sharply, her eyes imploring him to believe her. "I know exactly what I'm doing."

"Well, of course," said Thomas, "never met anyone more intelligent in my life."

They eyed each other in utter disbelief.

Zanny and Dolly had been in the police station waiting room for nearly half an hour before Sergeant Thomas sent for them. Constable Williams had informed him with intense glee that he'd better turn his collar back to front and take instruction from the local priest. "You are wasted on Zion," he said. "You are wasted in the police. A monastery for you, Thomas, and a hair shirt. Two more from the convent out there – like bees to honey they come."

Thomas had reminded him, rather sharply for him, that he was speaking to a superior officer. Williams had winked cheekily.

"If it's lost bikes – lost pumps – or lost pedals," Thomas said, "then why pass it to me?"

Williams made a noose of his fingers and placed them

around his neck. He rolled his eyes upwards and pretended to choke. "Murphy," he said.

Mother Benedicta had said one. She hadn't said three. Thomas told Williams to give him ten minutes and then to knock on his door with a plausible story. It was nearly lunch time.

He had expected two more elderly ladies and was surprised to see a very beautiful young girl with golden hair accompanied by a less beautiful but still quite interesting companion of about the same age. The beautiful one looked as if she had recently been weeping. The less beautiful one was frowning. Thomas told them to sit down. They obeyed in silence.

"Well?" said Thomas.

"I killed Bridget," said the beautiful one. "And I thought you ought to know."

"Well – now," said Thomas, leaning back in his chair.

He looked at the less beautiful one. "And you killed Bridget, too?" he suggested blandly.

"I most certainly did not," said Dolly indignantly.

Zanny, who had spent most of her waking hours visualising this scene, felt as if she had walked into a glass box. There was nothing in it. No response. No start of horror. No narrowing of the eyes in appraisal. Absolutely nothing. Instead a cool elderly policeman, old enough to be her grandfather, was smiling at her quizzically. It really would not do.

Dolly was the first to understand the situation. She read newspapers whenever she could get hold of them. She read news reviews and books, both fact and fiction.

"It's quite obvious to me," she said, in what she hoped was a good counsel for the prosecution tone, "that you don't believe my friend."

"Well now," said Thomas, who had been patient for quite a long time and was getting rather tired of it, "you might well be right."

"Confessions, I suppose," said Dolly, "in a case like this, are thick on the ground."

134

"Like daisies in summer-time," said Thomas.

"I put it to you," said Dolly, "that amongst the daisies there might be an acorn of truth."

"Unlikely," said Thomas, looking at her with a degree of interest.

"In this particular case," Dolly said, "there is more than an acorn – there is a whole tree." She was sorry she had used the metaphor, but having used it decided to carry on with it. "Felons," she said, "are hanged on trees. In this case the wrong felon."

A conversation of long ago came back into her mind – and into Zanny's – something about little Willie and apples hanging on trees.

"My friend," said Dolly, "murdered my brother when she was six – she murdered Mr. Evans, the breadman, shortly after, by making him crash his van – and now, quite recently, she murdered Bridget O'Hare."

"Friend – is it?" said Thomas.

"For want of a better word," said Dolly.

Thomas began actively to dislike the less beautiful one. He had seen cases of intimidation in his time and was quite convinced he was seeing one now. Bullying went on in most schools, but this surely was carrying it too far.

"If you have a complaint to make," he said gently to Zanny, "then don't be afraid to make it to me. It would have been much better to have gone to Mother Benedicta first, but as you haven't . . . or have you?" Zanny shook her head. "Then tell me why your – your – companion – is bullying you."

"Oh, but she's not," said Zanny, surprised. 'We have to leave the convent in twos – and she's the only one who knows all about it – I wanted her to come."

"It takes courage," Dolly said, "to confess to murder."

"Any confession this young lady makes," Thomas said, "she will make when you are not around to intimidate her. Go outside."

Dolly, surprised, was about to argue but changed her

135

mind. In days to come men like Thomas would grovel at her feet. If it pleases your Worship, they would say . . .

"Out!" said Thomas, holding the door open for her.

And now for thumb screws, Zanny thought. We are alone. I am at his mercy. The silky, kindly ones were the worst. Her eyes filled with tears. Oh, Murphy, Murphy, I am doing this for you. I feel sick. I need to go to the lavatory. I love you.

"There is no need to be afraid," Thomas said. "Of anyone. When I was a little lad in school, I got pushed around until I learnt to fight. Young ladies don't fight, but they can be strong in other ways. You don't have to do everything that other young lady tells you."

Zanny, surprised at the route the conversation was taking, said that Dolly hadn't told her to do anything. "She left it to my conscience."

Devious, Thomas thought. Nasty. Too much poking around with a conscience left you with a guilt complex which this young girl quite obviously had.

"Whatever you've got to tell me," he said, "then tell it to me now – without fear. You won't be telling tales about the other young lady. It will just be the truth. If you are afraid of her, tell me – and tell me why. Everything will be all right. You are not to worry about anything."

Zanny, unable to make sense of the conversation, was beginning to shake. "Oh, but I am worried," she moaned, "so terribly worried. Murphy didn't kill Bridget. He's going to be hanged for something he didn't do."

Thomas didn't know much about psychology, but he knew that a guilt complex usually focussed on something. Murphy was in the news. A murderer awaiting execution was clothed in the minor sins of the unstable like a scarecrow. Miss Sheldon-Smythe, uncomplicatedly batty, had shone with resolve. This little girl was actually quaking with fright. He wondered what she'd done. Gone too far with a boyfriend, perhaps; she was old enough. And the other one had caught her at it? A little misdemeanour had blown up in her mind into a major catastrophe. The other one had played on her emotions like a flat-footed chapel organist with all the stops out. Of the two, she was the more unbalanced. Fancy saying this one had murdered Evans the Bread! What a cruel accusation! Though it was nine years ago he remembered the death of Evans quite clearly. He was his wife's cousin. Accident, the coroner had said. Well, obviously.

When people were upset they had to be calmed down. The other sadistic little madam had forced her to come here and talk a lot of nonsense. Well, he'd better listen.

"I killed Bridget O'Hare," Zanny said again. "I pushed her over the cliff. Murphy had nothing to do with it. You can't hang him."

Thomas sat back in his chair, wondering what to say that would make her feel better. "The world is full of bad people," he said, "and people who are not so bad who get caught up in bad situations."

"Bridget was bad," Zanny said. "She enticed Murphy. Murphy is a very good man."

"There is good in all of us," Thomas soothed.

"It was for Murphy's sake that I did it – that I pushed her over the cliff. He would never have been able to shake her off. She would have been around his neck for ever."

His neck.

Oh, Murphy!

"You've got to believe me. Don't I write a statement, or something? What do I do?" (She said it with a flash of anger and sounded like Miss Sheldon-Smythe.)

If it made her happy to write a statement, then she'd better write it. It was supposed to be good therapy to write things down. It was high time Mother Benedicta was told about all this. Not an easy case to handle. Adolescent girls were peculiar. When his own daughter

137

was this one's age she had run off to go on the stage and got as far as Liverpool. Lied like Lucifer, she had.

"Well, yes," Thomas said, pushing over paper and pen to Zanny's side of the desk. "Write it down, by all means."

My death warrant, Zanny thought, hesitating only momentarily. Well, it wasn't, of course. She wasn't sixteen yet. Her start of a new life, though – not a nice one.

She wrote the date in her rather spidery writing and then headed the paper with the convent address.

"I, Zanny Moncrief," she wrote, "being of sound mind and body did on" (she couldn't remember the date) "a day in early summer go up on the headland in Coracle Bay while on a school picnic and push Miss Bridget O'Hare over the cliff and into the sea where she died. Ignatius Murphy was not there when it happened. He has been falsely accused of Miss O'Hare's murder and must be set free."

She signed it Susannah Moncrief and put Zanny in brackets.

Just as she finished writing it, Constable Williams knocked at the door and came in. "There's an unexploded bomb in the backyard," he said.

Thomas, deploring his humour, and forgetting he had told him to rescue him in ten minutes, told him icily to leave them alone.

Then he read the statement through. "Good," he said, "very good indeed. Nice writing. Expressed very well."

"And now," said Zanny, "I suppose you'll arrest me." She felt very tired.

Thomas, too, was tired. It was proving very exhausting trying to explain why an arrest couldn't be made.

"Well, I wish I could," he said. "It's always so much easier to arrest people when you are a hundred per cent sure that you are doing the right thing. But I can't arrest you on this statement alone. There's got to be proof."

138

"What sort of proof?" asked Zanny.

"Well, somebody seeing you do it, maybe." He thought of the other one waiting outside. "And not your friend," he said hastily. "A complete stranger."

"You mean," Zanny asked aghast, "that if I can't produce a witness, Murphy will die?"

"Oh, I wouldn't say that," Thomas reassured her. "There's a petition going around the town asking for his reprieve. It will go up to the convent and you can put your name on it."

"Did anyone," Zanny asked, "say that they saw Murphy pushing Bridget O'Hare over the cliff?"

"Well – no – not exactly – no . . ." said Thomas. "It's circumstantial evidence in his case – no witness needed."

Zanny tried to clarify it. "So I would need a witness – and Murphy doesn't?"

"That about sums it up."

"I see," said Zanny, and she thought she did. Some people – such as herself – could kill with impunity. Some people carried the bugs of disease and didn't get it. Other people, who didn't carry the bugs, did. She, Zanny, could walk through a barrage of gunfire and because of her invisible protection didn't get hit. Murphy wasn't among the lucky ones.

Short of chaining herself to this chair like a suffragette to railings and refusing to budge there was nothing she could do.

"Well," she said. "I've told you."

"Yes," said Thomas, rising, "and you're not to worry any more."

"I think," Zanny said bitterly, "that you're mad."

"No doubt," Thomas replied, quite unruffled. "We're all a little mad. Given time we get better."

He saw her to the door.

This time the telephone call was from him to Mother Benedicta. She listened, appalled. When the old – such as Miss Sheldon-Smythe – were crazy, it was no great tragedy. But when the young started hallucinating it was serious. She thanked the sergeant for handling it so well. "Oh, I've gels of my own," he said comfortingly. "It's a funny time – adolescence – funny things happen."

Not an adjective I'd use, Mother Benedicta thought.

"The last time we had a murder in the town and the murderer was due to hang," Thomas said, "we had over twenty confessions. The death penalty does that to some people – upsets them, like."

Mother Benedicta was very sorry indeed that it had upset Zanny. As for Dolly's role – she just couldn't understand it. She was such a sensible, well-balanced girl. How extraordinary that she should aid and abet Zanny in this. And the Moncriefs had been so good to her – so very good. She decided to write to them. It would be easier to explain on paper. Nothing would be said about Dolly, of course. No point in jeopardising the child's future by antagonising her benefactors. If she was quick the letter would catch the late afternoon post.

Clare and Graham had just made love when the letter arrived. Contraception was no longer a contentious topic between them. Their one child, since the trial and conviction of Murphy, was proving one child too many.

Graham, on his way to the kitchen to put on the kettle for early morning tea, saw the envelope lying on the mat and brought it back to the bedroom. Clare, sleepy, naked, warm with love, was lying sated and happy under the sheet when she heard him tear it open. After a couple of minutes' silence while he read the letter she heard him give a little grunting moan.

"Income tax?" she asked, coming fully awake, "or the electricity bill?"

"Mother Benedicta."

More serious than either. She scrambled up onto her knees and read anxiously over his shoulder.

Mother Benedicta had been as tactful as she possibly

140

could be. She had started by saying what a pleasant, kind, very imaginative child Zanny was. "All the school," she had gone on, "were very disturbed indeed by the appalling tragedy of Bridget O'Hare and the subsequent sentencing of Murphy. I did what I could to minimise the shock of all this; banning newspapers and so on; but the truth couldn't be withheld altogether. Your very dear, very sensitive little daughter, shocked by the horror of the impending death of a man she had seen in the convent gardens (though, not to my knowledge had ever spoken to), became for a while emotionally unbalanced. Unknown to me (the excuse was a visit to the dentist), she went to the local police station and informed the station sergeant that it was she who had murdered Bridget."

"Christ!" said Clare.

She read on. "The sergeant, a sensible man well used to hearing several bogus confessions at times such as this, spoke a few kind words to her and sent her back to the convent. He then telephoned me and told me not to worry about it. Adolescent aberrations, he told me, were not new to him. They were best disregarded.

"I felt his advice was extremely sensible and as from now, obviously I had to tell you though I do regret having to worry you, I believe we should try to put it out of our minds.

"I reprimanded Zanny for going into the town on false pretences. I also told her quite sternly that she should keep her imagination on a tighter rein. She was quite upset at the time and kept insisting on her guilt. As the best way to calm a troubled mind is by filling it with hard work, I arranged for her class teacher to give her extra mathematics lessons. Her algebra is particularly weak. I also spoke to Father Donovan so that he might be prepared for a confession along similar lines. A minor penance for what is not only a lie but an emotional and rather unhealthy leaning towards martyrdom should convince Zanny of her folly.

141

"And so – Mr. and Mrs. Moncrief – having dutifully told you what I felt you should know – shall we now thank God for the sensitivity of a young girl and leave it with God.

"In a fortnight's time, on the fourteenth of this month, we are holding our Autumn Fair. It is to be opened by Sir Clifford Ponsonby who has recently come to live in the area. I hope as many parents as possible will attend and I shall look forward to your presence. By then I hope Zanny will be her usual cheerful self and that nothing need be said of what has happened."

Clare began to laugh. And then tears edged down her cheeks. "Bloody silly –" she said. She picked up the pillow and thrust it against her stomach.

Graham dropped the letter and watched it spiral to the floor.

Down below in the kitchen the kettle whistled. He walked down into the steam and made the tea. Today the office could go hang. Blast the word! He put the usual two biscuits on a plate and then the whole lot on a tray and carried it upstairs.

Clare was lying on her side in a foetal position with the pillow still pushed against her stomach, but when he came in she sat up and took the cup from him. She asked him what they were going to do.

He didn't know. At the end of the trial he had half believed in Murphy's guilt. A fifty per cent belief in Zanny's innocence had been comforting. He needed to cling to the comfort. The letter had posed a problem. Like a deep, sinister pool, it was best skirted around while he thought.

"We never knew for sure," he said, "that Zanny drowned little Willie."

He hoped that Clare would see it as a life-line across the pool and use it that way without plunging both of them in. He went on quickly. "Evans the Bread died accidentally. Okay – Zanny pushed Dolly. She might not have realised the van was so near. Children fall into

142

ponds. Children push children. Murphy had a good reason for getting rid of Bridget – why take it for granted he didn't do it? We didn't see Zanny drown Willie. No one saw her push Bridget. It seems to me we've been in too much of a hurry all these years to see the bad side of her – the bad side that probably doesn't exist."

"Then why did she make the confession to the police?" Clare's little tug on his life-line was malevolent.

He pulled back hard. "To quote Mother Benedicta – a desire for 'martyrdom'."

They looked at each other. And then they looked away.

"If we back Zanny's confession," Clare said, "Murphy will live."

"And what will happen to Zanny?"

Something indescribably awful, Clare thought. My womb cries out in protest.

"If I were religious," she said, not answering the question, "I'd leave this one with God. Either He'll let her get away with it – by not letting anyone believe her confession – or He won't."

"And as you're not religious?" (If you welsh on Zanny, much as I love you, Clare, I'll kill you.)

She took a biscuit and ate it slowly, letting crumbs drop on the sheet. (And if you welshed on her, I expect I'd do the same to you.)

"I'm quite prepared," she said at last, "to be temporarily converted."

The rope over the pool stayed taut. And then, their tension easing very slowly, they moved cautiously back from the brink.

On the whole, they decided, it would be wiser not to go to the convent fair. Zanny, wearied by mathematics and calmed by minor penances, might by then have regretted her impulsive confession – but they couldn't be sure of it. It was one thing to keep silent when they were apart from her – quite another to be battered by the

143

truth which she might well scream at them. Silence then would strain them to the limit.

They didn't put it to each other quite like that. They disliked fairs, they said. Graham had met Clifford Ponsonby at a Rotarian lunch and hadn't been impressed. He couldn't hold his liquor for one thing, and had been retired from the Circuit earlier than usual.

"Retired from what?" Clare asked, making safe little stepping stones of conversation away from Zanny.

"The Northern Circuit," Graham told her. "He's a retired judge."

"Not the one that Murphy . . .?"

"Nothing to do with Murphy."

"Love me," Clare said, "again . . ." Conversation was treacherous. Only flesh on flesh could soothe the mind.

He doubted if he had the strength. But he tried. And he had. They lay body on body while the anguish and the guilt oozed safely away.

The invitation to Sir Clifford Ponsonby had been sent and accepted long before Murphy's trial. Had Mother Benedicta been gifted with foreknowledge she would have asked any other local dignitary to do the honours. At this stage, the days getting closer and closer to Murphy's execution, any link with the law, even the retired law, was unfortunate. The emotional climate was well above normal. School essays – not just Zanny's, who wasn't much good at writing anyway – reflected the situation in different ways. Love, pain, horror in different guises spilled out of fountain pens and into copybooks.

Zanny, on Dolly's advice, wrote to the Home Secretary begging for a reprieve. Mother Benedicta, after much hesitation, allowed the letter to be posted. The Home Secretary would probably get dozens of similar letters. Miss Sheldon-Smythe was bound to have sent one, too.

144

Zanny's letter to her parents made no mention of the subject of Murphy at all. She hoped very much that they would come to the fair, she told them. That she would be there to receive them, she very much doubted. Her faith in the Home Secretary was implicit. She had told him. He would act. Mother Benedicta would break the news to her parents and explain her absence. On the whole, it was better coming from Mother Benedicta.

In the meantime the convent prepared for the fair. The arts and crafts section was to be housed in the main hall. This included paintings and needlework. Zanny, forced into work therapy, not only struggled with algebraical equations and lost, she painted blue lupins in a pale pink vase against a background of purple. Dolly's "Yuk!" was fair comment.

Dolly's contribution was clues to a treasure hunt. Her first lot of clues were so abstruse that the treasure – a box of chocolates – would have remained hidden for ever. Sister Clemence had pointed out crisply that the public at large were for the most part simple-minded and to devise clues that they might have some chance of understanding.

Most of the outdoor activities were of the sort that could be brought in quickly, should it rain. There were bran-tubs and hoop-la and darts.

There was also a small tent full of rabbits in hutches. They looked appealing. They were cheap. As a way out of Mother Benedicta's problem it was brilliant.

Miss Sheldon-Smythe looked at them sadly. "Your master," she told them, "may not return to you, but I shall fight – fight – fight." She had her own plans for the day of the fair. She hoped it would be fine.

There was now less than a week to Murphy's execution. Zanny confessed to Father Donovan. "And don't give me three Hail Marys," she said, "as you gave me once before." It was cheeky. He forgave her. And gave her five. The Home Secretary hadn't answered. The local police were useless. The nuns were working her into the ground. She was tired. She was wan. She had never looked more beautiful.

The day of the fair was cloudless. Hot, golden sunlight poured from the autumn sky. The girls in their neat blue uniforms moved amongst the guests introducing parents and friends. Dolly, as usual, was included in several groups. She still told the occasional fantasy story about her dear dead parents, but for the most part was accepted for herself. Zanny, who had hoped by this day to be absent, mooched glumly on her own. Her parents had phoned Mother Benedicta explaining why they couldn't come. The excuse, a thin one about a weekend in London with friends recently returned from abroad Mother Benedicta accepted with barely concealed annoyance and passed along to Zanny. Zanny didn't care. She walked in a fog of depression. Her parents had pushed her off to France during the holidays – and now they were ditching her again. Well, let them. It didn't matter. So – the sun shone – well, let it.

These days of agony, Murphy told her in her mind, will pass. You must do nothing. Say nothing. Your courage is like a beacon that will blind my eyes in the last moments. I die for you. You must not die for me.

Oh, but I must, Murphy.

And I will. I will. I will.

"Your job," Sister Clemence, who was in charge of the smooth running of the fair told her, "is to keep an eye on the crafts table. As the day is so hot the opening ceremony and the Greek dance will take place out of doors. Afterwards the main doors will be opened. Make sure you get to your table in plenty of time – and be sure you read the prices on the tickets. Do not reduce anything until late afternoon, and then only if certain items fail to sell. Anything that doesn't sell, even at a reduction, must *not* be given away. All the items will keep and there will be other fairs. Point out the quality of the stitching – stress the charities that will benefit – be an excellent salesgirl for the greater glory of God."

"I don't see why," Zanny said, "I – we – any of us – should be bothered with such trivial matters now."

"The world is made up of trivial matters," Sister Clemence told her. "It's like good, plain bread and butter – we survive on it."

"Some of us survive," said Zanny.

Sister Clemence and all the other nuns had been warned by Mother Benedicta to handle Zanny Moncrief with tact. Sister Clemence was tactfully tactless in French. "*Voyons, ne dis pas de bêtises!*" she said brusquely.

The main convent gates had been open for twenty minutes before Sir Clifford Ponsonby and his wife, Betty, drove up in their battered old Bentley. The fact that he was using the Bentley rather than the Rolls was an indication of his annoyance at having to attend this tin-pot occasion at all. He would have politely declined the invitation to open the wretched affair if he had had his way. But Betty wanted to come. Betty, large, florid, dominating, had engineered his rise to the top of the legal profession. She had pushed – pulled strings – steered – and heaved. His knighthood, she had told him, was due to her. But then his enforced retirement was also due to her: you lived with Betty and you drank. Or you left her. She had learned to put up with the drink provided he didn't make it too obvious. The flask in his hip pocket was nicely concealed. She reminded him about his speech.

"And don't mention Attlee and the Labour government."

"The world," he groaned, "has gone mad. I am mad. I live in a bungalow in the wilds of Wales. I launch lifeboats. I open libraries. I preside at bloody fairs in

147

bloody convents. How in Hades do I address the nun in charge?"

"Ma Mère is usual," Betty said with a touch of humour, "but probably not suitable for you. Try Reverend Mother – or just plain You. Keep your speech short. Don't be too mean with your money. And . . ." catching sight of the rabbit tent as they drove past it, "don't buy any of those."

It was one of the parents who told Dolly that Sir Clifford was a retired judge. Mother Benedicta had skilfully avoided mentioning it when explaining to the girls who was to do the honours this year. Dolly immediately sought Zanny out and told her.

"He might have influence with the Home Secretary."

By this time, Sir Clifford and his wife were standing by the tea tent on the top lawn in a little roped off area. From here he was to make his opening speech.

Zanny looked at him in some surprise. A retired judge? That little football of a man? He had purple cheeks. Very little hair. Large pink hands. No doubt the wig and gown would improve him, but not much. Did men like that – pig-like creatures like that – have the power of life and death over beautiful men like Murphy?

"It gives me very great pleasure" – he was lying suavely – "to be here in this lovely convent garden on this perfect autumn day. You do me great honour, Reverend Mother, by inviting me to attend your annual fair, and even greater honour by asking me to open it. As you know, I have recently come to live in the district after spending many years in Liverpool. I find the countryside a delight – and the people charming. My wife and I have been received everywhere with much warmth and excellent hospitality. Today I hope we shall make new friends amongst the pupils, their parents, and the local townspeople. The proceeds of the fair, I am told, go to various charities. May I present you, Reverend Mother, with a small preliminary con-

And then the tempo quickened. Robina, obeying instructions she was afraid to refuse, nodded nervously at
the orchestra. A senior girl, obeying the cue, joined the
orchestra with a pair of cymbals.

There was silence for twenty seconds.

Miss Sheldon-Smythe, as always totally clad in
black, walked into the centre of the dancers. They took a
step back from her, giving her room. She pointed an
imperious finger at the cymbals. They clashed.

Mother Benedicta, who had seen the rehearsal and
knew that this had nothing to do with it, stiffened with
apprehension. Sister Agnes had been told to stay with
Miss Sheldon-Smythe as much as possible and see
that she didn't make a nuisance of herself. Obviously
having given her the slip she was about to do just that.

Miss Sheldon-Smythe called out in a high reedy
voice, "Who do we want?"

The Greek dancers shouted, "Murph . . . ee . . ."

"How do we want him?"

"Free – free – free – "

The cymbals crashed three times.

It was repeated.

"Who do we want?"

"Murph . . . ee . . ."

"How do we want him?"

"Free – free – free."

The days of cheer-leaders hadn't arrived, but Miss
Sheldon-Smythe knew what she was doing. Instinct as
old as time prompted her. She wasn't a rabble raiser,
but she knew the tricks. Twelve Greek dancers
wouldn't make enough noise, but they would form a
very effective prelude to a beautifully orchestrated
crescendo.

"Who do we want?" She addressed the pupils directly, her eyes little burning points of fire – her voice
as loud as she could make it.

"MURPH . . . EE . . ." they yelled back, beginning to
sway with hysteria.

"How do we want him?"

"FREE – FREE – FREE," they screamed.

She raised both arms, fists clenched, her head thrown back, her mouth a defiant oval of pain and resolution. With the pupils on her side, their parents would have to start taking notice.

"Who do we want?"

It went on – and on – and on –

Some of the girls were wailing and crying. One had flung herself on the grass and was scrabbling at it with her nails.

Zanny, aghast, stood silently and watched. She felt as if she were being flayed alive. Dolly, slightly amused, stood at her side. She hadn't uttered either.

Mother Benedicta, long ago in her youth, had got caught up in a hysterical mob when a hotel had caught fire and the main exit doors had stuck. Young as she was then, she had managed to keep calm. She struggled to be calm now. She explained in a quick aside to Sir Clifford what it was all about. "I'm extremely sorry," she shouted in his ear, "but I don't know how to stop it." Usually her presence, a few sharp claps of the hands, sufficed. This time more was needed.

Sir Clifford, who had on one or two occasions cleared courts, wasn't intimidated. This occasion which only hours ago had threatened to be extremely boring was turning out to be anything but.

"My dear good lady," he shouted back at Mother Benedicta, "leave it with me."

Very few noticed him strolling over to the group around Miss Sheldon-Smythe. There was nothing belligerent in his approach. It was cool. Easy. Her eyes were closed now and her voice was hoarse with effort.

"Madam," he said, touching her on her right shoulder. "Madam."

He could feel the muscles tremble under her black cardigan as her raised arm began reluctantly to fall.

151

She opened her eyes and turned and looked at him. Her action today had burnt her boats for ever. The convent would request her departure. She had nowhere to go. The future had never been more bleak. She had never felt more fulfilled.

He wouldn't believe her, but she had to tell him. "I killed Bridget," she croaked.

His small, blue, piggy eyes were almost compassionate. When elderly women went off their rockers it wasn't very pleasant. It certainly wasn't funny. An elderly priest was joining them. As if he were presenting Miss Sheldon-Smythe to him in marriage, Sir Clifford took her hand and placed it on Father Donovan's. "Go," he said.

In the sudden silence everyone watched. The ring of dancers fell away as the old man in black led the old woman in black across the lawn, up the steps to the gravelled area in front of the main doorway, and then through the main door. It closed behind them.

Sir Clifford returned to Mother Benedicta and his wife and this time it was he who raised his hands in control. "Please!" he said, his voice resonant in the continuing silence.

Everyone looked at him. Tears still rolled down some cheeks. Breath came raggedly in tired breasts.

"You may know," Sir Clifford said, "that for many years I was a judge on the Northern Circuit. In that time many prisoners have appeared before me. Some innocent. Some guilty. It is a great responsibility to have a man's life in one's hands. It is a power that none of us wish to have. It is thrust upon us. It is a duty. Here in this beautiful convent you have very little knowledge of the outside world. You are young. You are idealistic. You see no evil in anybody. Let me convince you of this: the law of the land is there for your protection. It is fair. It is just. The law is on the side of the just – on your side. It is on the side of the weak – your side. It is on the side of the vulnerable – the kind – the good . . . your side. The law is on the side of Bridget O'Hare. Young – vulnerable – good – sadly done to death in the days of her joy. It is not on the side of her brutal murderer. Keep your compassion for those who deserve it. Bridget's family. Her friends. But for Murphy – Iggy Murphy – Bridget would be here amongst us on this lovely day. She would be standing beside you now. Would you have Murphy kill her and survive? Would you want him to go on breathing this beautiful autumn air when she cannot? He came to this convent and abused the trust placed in him. He acted with horrific savagery. And now he has been removed from you. You are safe. Let others take the responsibility of what happens to him. Believe me, it will be merciful and quick."

It wasn't a bad speech, he thought, particularly as it was off the cuff and delivered sober. They were quite a bit calmer now. There was one extremely good looking girl in her middle teens on the edge of the crowd. She had quite the most fantastic golden hair he had ever seen. Her face was grave, very pale. She was looking directly at him, her eyes locked into his.

Reluctantly he looked away from her. "And now," he said briskly, "enjoy yourselves. I'm going to. You've done a marvellous job with your stalls. I hope all the parents – all the visitors – will spend very freely. Mother Benedicta, shall we begin?"

"I can never begin to thank you," Mother Benedicta said. "I'm sure," she added turning to Betty, "that you are extremely proud of your remarkable husband."

"Oh, yes," Betty said easily, "he functions in times of crisis very well." (He also drinks, womanises and can behave quite appallingly – even in court. Why do you suppose he retired at fifty-eight – for love of green fields and pastures new? Oh, no, Mother Benedicta – for love of the bottle – and girls in short white Greek tunics and small round bottoms.)

"Remember not to exert yourself," she told him kindly.

She caught Mother Benedicta's expression of enquiry and tapped her heart significantly.

"Nonsense," Sir Clifford said cheerfully, "never been fitter."

"You won't do any good there," Dolly said to Zanny. "You can put the Home Secretary out of your mind. All he'd tell him would be to tighten the rope." She added, "His delivery wasn't bad. For a man who looks like an animated plum he has a fairly decent voice."

"Don't you feel *anything*?" Zanny asked. In the depths of her stomach was a deep hard pain. Iggy! How dare he use that dreadful diminutive! How dare he debase Murphy – make him sound like an animal! I'll get you, she thought, *I will get you.*

It was Dolly's job to start the treasure hunt. She told Zanny she would see her some time. "Aren't you supposed to be guarding your stall?"

Zanny was.

Miss Sheldon-Smythe's passionate involvement in Murphy's cause had come as a great shock to her. As she walked over to the main hall she kept thinking about it. It was an intrusion. Miss Sheldon-Smythe was poaching on her preserves. Murphy belonged to her. He didn't – had never – belonged to Miss Sheldon-Smythe. She, Zanny, should have been standing in the middle of the dancers yelling for Murphy. She hadn't thought of it. Miss Sheldon-Smythe had taken a march on her. She had presumed. She had a colossal cheek.

Deeply jealous of her initiative, Zanny stood gloomily behind the large table set out with ridiculous objects. Who but a fool would buy egg-warmers knitted in white wool with faces on them? And who but a fool would mark them at one and nine pence halfpenny? How much was that from ten shillings? And look at these mats made from straw – hideous things. And a string shopping basket. String – child of rope.

"How much," said a voice, "is this pen-holder?"

Zanny looked up with glazed eyes. "I've no idea," she

said at last. "Whoever is running this stall will be here soon." She was about to walk out when she saw Sister Clemence walking in. "As a matter of fact," she said, in deep anger at being trapped, "it's one and eight pence, and it's no use brandishing that pound note at me, I haven't any change."

Towards four o'clock Sir Clifford found his way into the reception hall. This was adjacent to the main hall and was used for entertaining visitors when the parlour was in use. It was full of potted palms and wicker chairs. He had noticed its seclusion earlier and marked it for a future retreat. Father Donovan had recently waylaid him in the tea tent and given him a surreptitious drop of what he called the hard stuff. Father Donovan was very grateful for his tactful handling of Miss Sheldon-Smythe. The poor lady, he said, was now lying down in her room with one of the nuns in attendance. She was, the judge understood, didn't he, unwell? Yes, said Sir Clifford, he understood. His understanding had been further rewarded by Father Donovan with a glass of what looked like pure lemonade, but wasn't. The problem was that no more had been forthcoming and it was easier not to drink at all than to drink a little. Father Donovan's generosity was limited by circumspection, but at least he still had his own hip flask. He had just downed most of its contents, tactfully hidden by one of the palms, when he noticed the smasher with golden hair sitting in the far corner by the window watching him.

His embarrassment was fleeting.

His embarrassment equated with the degree of his sobriety.

"Hello, pussy," he said.

"Hello," said Zanny.

She had not been stalking him. She had not had him in mind. She had come here because she had been banished from her stall. She had a vague impression

155

that the academic standards of the convent were likely to fall into grave disrepute if she were to stay at her stall any longer. Sister Clemence had overheard derogatory comments, Sister Clemence had told her. Was she a child of five who couldn't add up or take away? Didn't she know that one and four pence and three and eight pence made five shillings and that if you took that from a pound there were fifteen shillings left? She didn't. Neither did she care. "You may be under strain," Sister Clemence scolded her sharply, "but so are we all. For goodness sake, go and get yourself another job – the bran-tub, perhaps, at tuppence a time."

"Having a rest?" asked Sir Clifford.

"Yes," said Zanny.

"Me too," said Sir Clifford, ungrammatically, but chummily. "I get a bit breathless – need to sit now and then. Ever heard of Anno Domini?"

"A saint?" asked Zanny.

"Devil, more likely," said Sir Clifford. "Has power over the arteries. These days I live in a bungalow – no stairs. Have you ever considered how crassly bourgeois a bungalow is?"

Zanny hadn't.

Pig, she thought. Pig. Pig. Pig. Hang Murphy, would you? Pig. Pig. Pig. All the resentment that had burned in her after his speech was being rekindled with every word he spoke.

"Has anyone ever told you what remarkably pretty hair you have?" asked Sir Clifford, edging his chair a little nearer.

"Frequently," said Zanny. She had been aware of her good looks for quite a long time.

There was a smell in the air, rather like the smell in Murphy's cottage that night she had gone to him. The smell – unpleasant – she had managed to banish from her mind most of the time. His missing tooth – the one small flaw – she had learnt to disregard. Perfect beauty was a bore. Murphy was never that.

Oh, Murphy, be boring. Wear a pinstriped suit. Work in an office. Don't have a body that glows. Be dull. Be dim. Be free.

"Murphy," she said, "is innocent."

The judge had no intention of getting on to that again. "Balls," he said briefly and rudely, recovered himself and apologised.

Zanny, not understanding the expression, shrugged. If you were put through a mincer, she thought, you would come out as sausage meat.

An intense little female, Sir Clifford thought. Pretty breasts, not too big. Nice thighs under that dress. Has she got it hooked up on the cushion on purpose or doesn't she know.

Zanny, following the direction of his gaze, wriggled her dress down over her knees.

Disappointed, Sir Clifford took a piece of paper from his pocket. "A clue," he said, "from the treasure hunt. Clue Number Five. 'Ask old Father Time'."

"Rather easy, wouldn't you say?" said Zanny.

"The grandfather clock by the entrance to the concert hall?" suggested the judge. "I was on my way there when I stopped off to rest."

An idea was forming in Zanny's mind.

"Not that clock," she said, "that one is comparatively new. Old Father Time refers to a very old clock on the landing." (The top landing, near the dormitory, where the stairs are steep.)

"Oh," said Sir Clifford. "Well, stairs are out for a start. You wouldn't like to nip up and get the clue for me, would you?"

"I'd be only too happy to help," Zanny's voice was less hard now, more silky, "but that would be cheating, wouldn't it? It would go against my conscience."

"And you have a very delicate conscience?"

"Depending," said Zanny.

Were her eyes turning a soft, almost milky blue or was that his imagination?

157

"Depending on what?"

"Some things matter," Zanny said, not quite sure what she meant, it was the tone of voice that counted, "and some things don't. I'd be prepared to do quite a lot of things for people I like."

She would be prepared to do quite a lot of things. He had heard that before from different sources. Mature sources. How old was she? Sixteen? Was he being over-optimistic if he risked seventeen?

"But you wouldn't cheat?"

"No."

"So you wouldn't help me?"

"Oh, I'd help you. I'd go with you." Zanny turned her head and looked at the ceiling. "Upstairs," she said.

Did she mean what he thought she meant? Or was it the whisky talking in his mind? The whisky tended to talk a lot of garrulous nonsense – garrulous and delightful nonsense.

He smiled at her. "Pretty pussy," he said. It was just a feeler.

"*Miaw*," said Zanny, making contact.

He sat still for several minutes, excitement rising inside him. He had done a lot of stupid things in his time, but nothing this stupid. You didn't open a convent fair and then lay one of the pupils. But wouldn't you, said the whisky, given the chance? No, said the judge, it's unthinkable – certainly not.

He edged the chair back.

Zanny was pleating her dress. She was pulling it up and down over her knees as she pleated it. She had never seduced anyone in her life, but for the first time it wasn't a bad effort. She looked over at Sir Clifford and smiled shyly.

Innocent as a raindrop, he told himself and didn't believe it.

"Well –" he said, "if it isn't far up the stairs . . ."

"Not very," said Zanny, "and we can take it as slowly as you like."

Take what slowly? he thought. How knowledgeable was she? Suzanne, the French wife of a junior counsel, was the slowest player of the game he knew. *Largo* for a very long time and then a thundering *prestissimo* conclusion.

They hadn't got a very long time.

He was a highly respected retired judge.

Well . . . respected by those who didn't know.

Retired by those who did.

"You stand," Zanny said, "a very good chance of winning."

"Winning? Winning what?"

"The treasure, of course," said Zanny. "Aren't you dying to know what it is?" Dying, judge – dying.

"Come," she said, "I'll show you."

"Show me?"

"The way."

The first flight of stairs – wide and shallow – she danced up, her skirt swirling tantalisingly so that he had glimpses of the backs of her knees – sweet little hollows. He laboured after her, the vicious hammer in his chest tapping at the hard metallic anvil in small warning blows.

"Hold on there," he said. "Hold on."

She turned on the top step and began creeping down. "Pussy," she said, "pussy."

"You – pussy," he said.

"You Tarzan – me Jane," said Zanny, three steps away from him.

The little devil. The little randy bitch. Where would she take him? Where would be private enough?

"Where?" he asked.

"Higher – higher – higher . . ." She pointed past the cool blue and white Virgin with the flowers around her feet, "Up – and around . . ."

"Far?"

"Not very."

"Heart sick."

"Poor sick heart."

"Pussy."

He hauled himself onto the half-landing. She disappeared around the corner and began walking up the second flight. He wanted to lie down on the parquet under the banked up flowers at the statue's feet. His forehead was cold and wet. What he was doing was mad. He should just sit down here for a few minutes – in the corner where the stairs turned. No one would see him. He needed to rest. He would then go down. Put the crazy episode out of his mind.

"*Miaw*," said Zanny. She was sitting half way up the second flight.

He shook his head. "No good. Can't."

Purple face, Zanny thought. Purple hangman. Call him Iggy, would you? Not let him breathe the autumn air, would you?

"Oh, come," she said gently, very adultly, "come – do come – try – do try . . ."

His breath was like flames.

He closed his eyes.

She was humming a little tune to herself. "The Roses of Picardy". He raised his head and looked at her. She had opened the top buttons of her dress. Her left nipple showed like a tiny pink rosebud.

He groaned.

He began climbing again.

One step up the mountain – two steps – three.

Twelve in all. He had reached the second landing.

The hammering in his chest was making all his bones ache – his arms – his wrists – his finger-tips. He was in a furnace of pain. And through it all he kept on desiring her.

White clouds at the top of the mountain. Huge pillows. Flesh, white as sugar crystals – sweet as sugar crystals.

"Sugar," he moaned.

"Honey," said Zanny. She had taken off her shoes.

160

Her feet were near his forehead. Not yet. Not yet. Not steep enough. The third flight.

He began crawling across the second half-landing as she crouched in front of him, urging him on.

He was quite mad. He was sane enough to know he was quite mad. He was mad. He was drunk. He should stop this minute while there was still time. He stopped and rolled over on his side. He would lie still while his breath raged through him like a wind across a burning desert.

She leaned over him – cool – smiling.

"Crawl a bit – lie a bit – ?"

He crawled a bit. Lay a bit. He couldn't ask how much further it was. He couldn't speak at all. He was beginning to forget why he had come this far. There was another mountain . . . blacker . . . higher . . .

Her feet were in front of him all the time. Up a few steps they went. He crawled up one step. Down a few steps came the feet. They touched his forehead – gently – softly.

"Up," said a voice that seemed to come from a very long way. "Pussy – pussy – pussy – pussy – up – up – up – up – "

The side of the mountain was jagged with rough rocks that were pressing into his flesh. An avalanche of cold water – could it be his sweat? – was washing into his eyes. He was almost at the top now. Almost – but not quite.

"*Miaw*," Zanny encouraged, "*miaw – miaw* – pretty pussy – *miaw*."

She put on her shoes.

Down in the main hall Mother Benedicta and the judge's wife heard what they interpreted as a mewling cry of fear. They looked up and in the distance saw the judge nearing the top step of the top landing. They didn't see Zanny's sudden kick. It was doubtful if the judge felt it. He had begun falling into a black pit before she touched him. And then he fell in reality, his rotund body slithering from step to step. The half-landing, highly polished, gave his descent momentum; he skidded across it, and thumped down the second flight, his head beating against the banisters in sharp cracks. The flower-pots around the Virgin halted him on the first landing. His dead eyes peered through fuschia petals like small helpless slugs.

Zanny slowly descended.

One for you, Murphy.

She felt like a sponge that had been squeezed. Her legs began to tremble and her jaw shook as if she wanted to cry but couldn't.

They were with him now. Mother Benedicta and his wife. His wife had moved him away from the flowers and had put him to lie flat. She had her ear to his chest. She was very calm. She looked at Mother Benedicta and shook her head. Mother Benedicta's cheeks looked as if someone has taken a dollop of rouge out of a jar and rubbed it all over them. And now the rouge was paling off – draining away in patches.

Zanny went and stood beside them. "Is he dead?"

Mother Benedicta turned and looked at her. She looked particularly hard at her open dress and then with fumbling fingers buttoned her up into respectability.

"Yes," she said.

"I killed him," Zanny said. This time there were witnesses. Two of them. This time Sergeant Thomas would be satisfied. This time there would be no doubt about it at all. They would believe she had killed Bridget. Murphy would go free.

"You understand, don't you," she said quite clearly, despite the fact that her jaw still shook, "that I killed him?"

"You poor shocked child," said the judge's wife, surprisingly. She stood up and held Zanny in her arms. "My husband," she said, "could behave very foolishly. I hope he didn't frighten you. I hope he didn't hurt you. I noticed your dress . . ." she held Zanny a little away from her and looked at her with deep concern.

"He didn't touch me," Zanny said truthfully.

"I appreciate your saying that," Betty said. "I appreciate it enormously."

And then she began to cry – and so did Zanny. They wept, for different reasons, each in the other's arms.

Six

*I*magination, Father Donovan thought, could be a terrible thing. Fortunately, Murphy was relatively free of it. Take his choice of books, for instance. Father Donovan had made a point of keeping him well supplied with reading material – mostly *The Farmer* and *Stockbreeder* and innocuous stories of the saints. If the saints were also martyrs – and quite a lot of them were – Father Donovan did some careful editing. The horrific sufferings of others tended to heighten one's fear of one's own impending doom – or so Father Donovan argued. When Murphy, who read very little anyway, asked for a collection of Sexton Blake stories Father Donovan had held out for as long as he could. Not that he read them himself or knew much about them apart from the dust-jackets which were bloody in the extreme. On his visit this week he had chosen the mildest-looking one he could find – a gloved hand with a gun in it. He had also included copies of the *Dandy* and *Beano*. That a grown man should read comics had come to him as a surprise. But Murphy did. Murphy had requested them. He had also requested a book on the Irish potato famine by an author he couldn't remember. Father Donovan, drawing a blank here, gave him his own copy of Sean O'Casey's *Juno and the Paycock*. Murphy received it politely and without enthusiasm. He had seen it on stage in Dublin. He hadn't liked it. Booze and the Troubles were serious matters. No joke.

Neither was his being here a joke.

Most of the time he couldn't believe it.

He must, surely to God, be in the depths of an alcoholic nightmare.

"Well, Murphy," said Father Donovan, falsely bright, "and how are you, this day?"

"All right," said Murphy.

"Sleeping?" asked Father Donovan.

"'Tis an explanation," said Murphy.

Small talk in these horrific circumstances was difficult. Father Donovan told him about Miss Sheldon-Smythe's behaviour at the convent fair. "Sure, she nearly had everyone marching here to get you out."

"Nice old biddy," said Murphy, surprised and rather pleased. Father Donovan's tittle-tattle about the convent was usually a bit of a bore.

The next item wasn't boring either. Father Donovan told him about the judge. "It seems he climbed some stairs" (no reason given) "and fell. The coroner at the inquest said it was a massive heart attack."

Murphy brightened perceptibly. It was an act of treason for Mother Benedicta to get a judge to open the fair. It was an act of God to kill off the old bugger.

"Good," he said.

Father Donovan's gentle elderly face creased in disapproval and then smoothed out again into understanding. If he, Father Donovan, were sitting here with the sure and certain knowledge that the hangman had viewed him at some stage – probably during his period of exercise – and assessed his weight and all the other disgusting details connected with an execution – then he, too, might regard the death of Ponsonby without sympathy.

"It's a pity," Murphy said, "it wasn't the bloody punk of a judge who set me up at my trial."

Father Donovan struggled to be silent and lost. "My son," he said, "'tis a state of grace you should be aiming for. Will you not confess it to me now?"

Murphy listened to a burst of birdsong just outside the barred window of the visitors' room. It reminded him of his hens. He wondered who was looking after them. He wondered, too, who would look after the auld

165

fellow in Ireland in the days of his dotage – not too far in the future. It occurred to him very forcibly that he wouldn't be around himself to do so. He was in no great hurry to reach a Catholic heaven, full of rabbits and a celestial Bridget. (Would Bridget's unborn baby go to Limbo? He wasn't well up on this sort of thing.)

A sudden spasm of fury shook him. He had done nothing. He was here for something he didn't do.

"If I had a bomb," he said, "I'd explode it."

"May the Blessed Virgin forgive you."

"Oh, she would," Murphy said with the supreme conviction of his faith, "she most surely would."

"You still insist you didn't kill Bridget?"

"May the Lord strike me dead this minute if I did," said Murphy.

It would be a kindness, Father Donovan thought, either way. He had arranged with the prison authorities to hear Murphy's last confession when the time came. And the time was coming rapidly. His own courage had never been put to the test in this way before. He had visions of passing out on the floor at Murphy's feet. Man's inhumanity to man had never ceased to appal him. Had he been told to witness the crucifixion of Christ he would have rushed howling off into the wilderness.

Murphy was no Christ.

But neither was he Barabbas.

Of that he was sure.

On his return to the convent he went to see Mother Benedicta to report on his visit. Murphy wasn't looking too bad, he told her. He had made a complaint about the dinner he'd had that day – braised hearts. Though he wasn't a fastidious eater, Murphy drew the line at hearts. He had given him some books. They had talked. He had insisted on his innocence. The prison authorities had sliced through the middle of the cake the nuns had baked him in case there was anything in it.

"Such as what?" asked Mother Benedicta acidly, "a gun – a file – ?"

"Such as a wee small bottle of plum brandy which had passed through on another occasion," Father Donovan said, without apology.

Mother Benedicta in an attempt not to smile sucked in her lips sharply. Father Donovan's kindness wasn't always selective. If the devil himself had been committed to the flames in front of him, the old priest, as like as not, would extend his hand into the furnace and try to haul him out.

"Come with me to the art room," she said. "There's something I must show you."

The art room was on the top floor. It was north facing and was lit by a wide window and a skylight. The art teacher, Sister Elizabeth, had once had a picture in the Royal Academy and knew what she was about. As well as the more usual work on easels she liked her pupils to use the large expanse of white walls for a mural. The present mural, depicting the story of King Arthur, was the painstaking work of two terms. All that was left of it was a clenched fist holding Excalibur. The sword pointed to a black rectangle of paint in the middle of the blue lake. In the rectangle painted in red were the words: "I killed Bridget, signed Zanny Moncrief". And underneath in even larger letters of yellow: "NONSENSE, I DID! signed AGATHA SHELDON-SMYTHE".

"Miss Sheldon-Smythe is now on her way to a rest home in Bournemouth," Mother Benedicta said, "I suppose you could call this her final parting gesture."

"And the child?" asked Father Donovan.

Zanny Moncrief's lunacy was of a more temporary nature, Mother Benedicta believed. "She's not academically gifted," she said, "at anything. When I saw this, I reprimanded her, naturally, and . . ."

'And?"

"Arranged for her to have music lessons, in addition to the extra lessons in mathematics. Her parents recently bought her a piano. Music could be an emotional

167

outlet – mathematics, apart from being necessary, will instil discipline."

It was all typical of Mother Benedicta's good sense, Father Donovan thought. There was a pot of green paint on a nearby table. He couldn't resist it. He picked up a paintbrush, dipped it in the paint, and wrote *Mea Culpa* carefully underneath.

"And now," Mother Benedicta suggested crisply, "you can paint the whole lot out." The acknowledgment of personal sin was all very well, but there was a limit to everything. She'd had enough.

On the night before the morning on which Murphy was due to die she would send Zanny Moncrief home. Already hysteria was beginning to rise again – just as it had on the day of the fair. Some might even begin to believe that what the child was saying was true. She shuddered to think what might happen to her. Luckily none of the girls had seen this piece of graffiti. She stood with arms folded as Father Donovan energetically sloshed green paint over the lot.

"I intend to have a very serious talk with her parents," she told him.

Music therapy included listening to records. Zanny, listening in utter boredom to Handel's *Water Music*, wondered how she was going to break through the crust of disbelief that had grown around her. She felt like a wreck at the bottom of the ocean encrusted with barnacles. Nobody – except Dolly – believed a word she said. Dolly had asked her with a degree of respect how she had got rid of the judge. She had told her. She had kept on believing her even after the inquest. It had been Dolly's suggestion that she should paint a confession on the art room wall. Both girls remained unaware of Miss Sheldon-Smythe's nullifying confession painted under it.

Dolly, who had been dragooned into having extra music lessons with her (she could say clever things about symphonic form), had just suggested, *sotto voce*, that she might try writing a confession to the local weekly. As the Home Secretary had totally ignored her it was unlikely that a letter to a small local newspaper would do any good, but anything was worth trying. Dolly, pretending to write notes on musical appreciation, drafted it for her. Later that evening, after a blindingly boring and incomprehensible period trying to learn something called the binary system, Zanny copied it out. Obeying instructions from Mother Benedicta who had become very vigilant, the nun in charge of posting letters removed it from the pile and gave it to her. Mother Benedicta tore it up. She had relied on the Home Secretary's good sense – justifiably. As from now she decided not to rely on anyone's but her own.

The summons to the convent came as no surprise to Graham and Clare. The two inquests into the deaths for which Zanny was responsible had gone in her favour. Willie and Sir Clifford Ponsonby were nine years apart, but Zanny's hand was evident in both. They didn't say this to each other. During these last few days of Murphy's life they were saying very little at all.

If he dies, Clare was thinking, I'm as guilty as if I hanged him myself.

If he doesn't die, Graham thought, Zanny will – in one way or another. Words from the marriage ceremony floated into his mind. *For ever hold your peace.* One day, Zanny, when this is over, you'll undergo a miraculous change and become normal. You won't kill another living soul. You'll marry with a crown of orange blossom in your hair. And not a stain of blood on you anywhere. Except perhaps the ending of your virginity on your wedding night. That's your future, Zanny, if I keep my mouth shut. Which I will.

Anyway, we don't know for sure. We never have. And probably never will.

"Mother Benedicta thinks we should drug her," Clare said wanly.

"What?"

"When she phoned the other evening she suggested a sleeping pill on Murphy's last night. When she wakes up it will be all over."

"Oh, God!" said Graham.

He went out to clean the car. All the horrible jobs were being done. The lawns and flower-beds had never looked so neat. Clare had cleaned all the brass like a maniac. Music and mathematics for Zanny. Work exhaustion for him and Clare. Nothing worked. Sleeping tablets would be a good idea for all of them.

And for Murphy?

Christ!

Peter Tolliston had long since departed to a more lucrative medical practice in Yorkshire. His successor, Caradoc Davis, known familiarly as Doctor Caradoc to distinguish him from another Doctor Davis in the area, had been born in the Rhondda. In the more rarefied atmosphere of mid-Wales his pit language wasn't always appreciated. On the whole he had learned to tame it when conversing with women. But he wasn't pliable. He didn't believe in drugs. He spent a lot of his time, he told Clare, curing cures. Anyway, he said, looking at her intently, both she and Graham had been disgustingly healthy for years, so what was supposed to be the matter with her now?

She had come to see him without Graham. They were both in a highly emotional state, but of the two she was the calmer.

"I haven't come about myself," she told him. "It's about Zanny. She's desperately worried about the execution of the Irish gardener. You've read about the case?"

Caradoc had. The death penalty, he thought, was unusually severe. It had seemed like an impulse killing. The poor bastard had been unlucky with his judge and jury.

"One day," he said, "the judicial system will become more civilised."

Clare, sensing a grain of sympathy, went on to tell him her edited version. She used the word hallucinating a lot – also sensitivity and empathy, just to be on the safe side. "She thinks if she says she did it, then Murphy will go free. An elderly member of the staff has been emotionally affected in the same way. If you could give Zanny something to make her sleep the night before he dies . . ."

Caradoc had heard of his predecessor's liaison with Mrs. Moncrief. She was still a pretty woman. He didn't know the daughter. The convent doctor saw to her during term-time and she seemed to have been remarkably free of illnesses during the holidays. Emotional upsets sometimes came on with the onset of menstruation. He asked if she were menstruating.

Clare, wishing it were that simple, said that she was. "There's nothing wrong with her physically. She just needs a pill to calm her."

"Sleeping pills," Caradoc said, "are for geriatrics waiting for the Big Sleep. How old is Zanny?"

"Fifteen."

"You want me to pump pills into a kid of fifteen?"

"Just this once – please. Honestly, she needs them." (So do I.)

The unspoken plea made telepathic contact. He didn't understand. It was his nature to need to understand. He never did anything without considerable thought.

"Bring her to me," he said, "and I'll try to talk some bloody sense into her. Make it the end of the surgery – about seven-thirty."

"She's hysterical," Clare said alarmed. "She's likely to tell you the most appalling things."

"I am never appalled," Caradoc said. "If she needs the pills, I'll give them. If she doesn't, I won't. Satisfied?"

Clare wasn't, but she tried to be.

The last two days of Murphy's life were for him an artificial period in which he sat around brooding – or marched around the yard, brooding. As if time went full circle he was back in his childhood, snotty-nosed, scratched-kneed. He could smell the bark of the trees he climbed. His naked feet squelched through warm mud. His first sexual experience had been with the sister of his best pal. He had been afraid of her enormous breasts – they had kept getting in the way, pushing him up off her. She had giggled like a donkey braying. Bridget's breasts had been very nice.

Old Father Donovan, looking rather ill and every year his age, didn't seem to know how to talk to him. It was embarrassing having him here. It's not my fault, Murphy thought, that I'm here. And it's not my fault that you're here. What do you want me to confess to you? That I liked Bridget's boobs?

"Hope you had a decent dinner today," Father Donovan said desperately.

"Pretty good," said Murphy. "Chicken." The grub was getting better by the minute. He was reminded of those poor sods of geese who were forcibly fed so that sodding punks of judges could eat *pâté de foie gras*.

"There's no equality," Murphy said, "that's the trouble."

Father Donovan ready to profess red hot Communism – anything to soothe – agreed.

He wanted to clasp this man in his arms. He wanted to run like hell away from him. He wanted to weep and didn't dare.

Clare and Graham arranged to fetch Zanny on the Thursday evening before Execution Friday at just after six-thirty.

Mother Benedicta's timing would have been the envy of a psychiatrist. Tea was at half past four. Between five and five-thirty Zanny with the help of one of the nuns packed her suitcase. Between five-thirty and six the girls went to Benediction. (This could be a time fraught with emotion – or it could be soothed by a holy blessing – Mother Benedicta had to hope for the latter, and did.) At six Zanny was taken to her classroom for extra mathematics by Sister Clemence who had a stronger personality than her class teacher and wouldn't allow thoughts to stray. Zanny would stay with Sister Clemence until six forty-five. She would then come down to the parlour and meet her parents. If Mother Benedicta hadn't finished talking to them, she would wait outside. As her parents had arranged to take her to the doctor's surgery by half past seven – a half-hour's drive away – they would be careful not to be late.

A reluctance to confront Zanny marred the timetable by a deficit of ten minutes. Graham and Clare, subdued and pale, arrived at six-forty. Zanny hadn't come down to the parlour yet so it didn't much matter; even so Mother Benedicta was annoyed.

"Heavy traffic?" she asked frigidly.

"Pretty heavy," said Graham.

Mother Benedicta had a small speech ready. She came out with it. "The world," she said, "is full of insensitive people who can take the horrors of life and not much care. Your daughter is not one of them. At this time she is suffering quite acutely on Murphy's behalf. Tomorrow morning she will walk to the gallows with him – in her mind. If she can sleep through that appalling period I believe she will be able to accept his death and begin to heal. That's why I'm sending her home with you. She is your responsibility. Only your own doctor can take on the responsibility of giving her that sleep. Will he?"

"Yes, I think so," said Clare, "but he won't give her the pills without checking up on her first."

A sensible precaution, Mother Benedicta conceded, though perhaps a bit fussy in this instance. She had sounded out the convent doctor, Harry Williams, on the same subject. Any knock-out drops, he had told her, had

173

better be given to Murphy before the final drop. Doctors, generally speaking, were too familiar with death. They tended to trivialise it.

"All the nuns are praying for Murphy," Mother Benedicta went on. "I shall personally say a prayer for Zanny. A sensitive imagination can be a Cross. She will need a great deal of help to carry it."

"Yes," said Clare. (And Zanny is our Cross – will somebody please help us?)

"I had thought of sending Dolly Morton home with Zanny," Mother Benedicta continued, "but Dolly was quite firm in her refusal." Stark fear had shown briefly in Dolly's eyes – so briefly that Mother Benedicta had thought she had imagined it. Often a child could help another child, but in this particular case Dolly obviously wasn't up to it.

Not even with my bedroom door locked and bolted, Dolly had thought, would I spend Murphy's last night with Zanny. Look what happened to the judge.

"This is a family matter," she had said tactfully. "I really think it would be better for me not to be there – I mean better for Zanny and her parents."

"You're quite right," Mother Benedicta had said. Dolly usually was. Her one lapse – accompanying Zanny to the police station – had been forgiven.

Mother Benedicta was about to expostulate about the lateness of everybody when Zanny knocked on the door and came in. She had changed out of her uniform and put on a blouse and skirt. Over this she wore her lightweight raincoat and had put on her straw panama hat with the blue ribbon. Her satchel, bulging with homework given by Sister Clemence, was slung across her shoulder.

"Baby," Graham said with sudden emotion and went over and kissed her.

She responded coolly, like a sleep-walker. Her skin was very pale and her eyes were deeply shadowed. She looked scrubbed neat and young – and exhausted.

174

Even Clare felt a twinge of pity. "Hello, darling," she said.

"Hello, Mummy." Zanny lifted her face to be kissed. Clare kissed it.

"Now Zanny," Mother Benedicta said crisply, "you're having a long weekend at home – and your parents know the reason. It's no use telling them you murdered Bridget O'Hare. It's no use telling anybody. It's utter nonsense and no one is going to believe you. Nothing you say or do is going to help Murphy. Only the Blessed Lord can do that. Leave it with God, child, and have an easy mind."

Mother Benedicta, mindful of authority's burden, never kissed any of the pupils, but this time she made an exception. The dry touch of her lips on Zanny's brow was over almost before Zanny was aware of it. "God bless you," she said.

Kissed and blessed Zanny got in the back seat of the car with her small suitcase. Mummy and Daddy were sitting in the front like a couple of wax effigies. And then they began talking at once.

"Awfully nice to have you home for a few days," said Daddy.

"We're going to Doctor Caradoc's surgery on the way," said Mummy.

"To get you vitamins or something," said Daddy, "to put in your Ovaltine."

"Well, everyone has to try . . ." Mummy said abstrusely.

"I mean to say . . . well . . ." said Daddy.

"Yes . . . quite . . ." said Mummy.

"That's the way it is," said Daddy.

"*Shut up!*" said Zanny.

Startled, they did.

Caradoc had had a fairly heavy surgery and the last couple of cases had been really ill. He had forgotten about the Moncrief child and was about to lock up when he saw the Moncriefs arriving. Graham, he noticed, had the good sense to stay in the car. The child – child? – young very attractive schoolgirl, more like – was following her mother into the waiting-room. His receptionist glanced at her watch, sighed, and waved them in.

"I don't want to be here either," Zanny told her truculently. "For God's sake let's all go home."

She was on the edge of hysteria. During the last ten minutes in the car she had been repeating the twelve times table. "Twelve," Sister Clemence had said, "is the shillings and pence table. If you had known that you wouldn't have made such a fool of yourself at the craft stall. You need a good grounding in simple things. Now repeat after me . . ."

Caradoc saw the appeal in Mrs. Moncrief's eyes and responded to it. Instead of telling the unmannerly little madam to get the hell out, he told her to get the hell in. "You're late. You're doing me no favour by being here. So sit down over there."

He turned to Clare. "Problems?"

"She's very edgy." (And unusually rude.)

"You would be edgy," Zanny said sullenly, "if someone was going to die for you."

"Oh, the murder thing . . ." Caradoc snapped his fingers, remembering. He drew his chair up to Zanny's and faced her. "Everyone else takes the rap for you – is that it?"

"If you call being hanged taking the rap – yes," said Zanny.

"Murdered Bridget O'Hare, did you?"

"Yes – and others."

"There are better pastimes," Caradoc observed mildly.

He had just had two bad cases – this was his third. He was wise enough to acknowledge it. All right – give the kid time – she needed it.

"Tell me," he said.

"You won't believe me."

"Perhaps not, but tell me anyway."

176

She sat slumped in her chair and fixed her gaze a couple of inches above his head. An eye-testing chart on the opposite wall seemed to be full of Os like a noose. Her confession was like a small fire-arm letting off bullets. If she flagged he re-loaded the gun. Her aggression ran the whole gamut of sound from a whisper to a shout – and once she burst into tears. Clare, like a shrivelled up little ghost, listened in horror.

At the end of it Caradoc was as unimpressed with Zanny's truth as was everyone else. Willie and Bridget were almost believable – but not Judge Ponsonby. Respectable judges were not seduced by convent schoolgirls at convent fairs. No way! She had a high-grade technicoloured imagination and saw too many B movies. Just now she was in the middle of an X horror film and couldn't find her way out. She needed that night's sleep. Afterwards – for a while – she might need a shrink. A placebo would probably put her to sleep as well as anything – a physical examination might give her more faith in the dud pill. He told her to strip off to her vest and pants and get on the couch.

Zanny, snuffling with the catarrh that followed her tears, accepted the handkerchief that Clare handed her.

"Why," she asked, after she had blown her nose, "should I get on the couch?"

"Well, I'm not going to bloody rape you," Caradoc said, fetching his stethoscope. (One day your language will be your downfall, an outraged matron had told him once, but on the whole they liked it.)

Zanny, through her snuffles, was beginning to like it, too. He was the first real man she had met since Murphy. He was a few years older than Murphy and his hair was beginning to go at the top. But he had shoulders like an ox and he had all his teeth. His fingernails were clean and he smelt of surgical spirit.

He was putting the cold stethoscope on her warm flesh and telling her to breathe. She breathed – gave a little shudder – and breathed again. Now he had her on

177

her stomach and was listening at the back. Her body, until now cold-frozen with the horror of Murphy, warmed a little.

"Turn over again," he said, "I'm going to prod your stomach."

It was all quite unnecessary, but a good act. "The pill I'm going to give you," he said, "is a bloody marvel. You'll never sleep better in your life." He gave her stomach another push. "How does that feel?"

"All right," said Zanny. (Rather nice, actually. Don't stop.)

He stopped.

"Good. Get dressed. Go home. Stop being a nuisance. Okay – so you murdered Bridget – and others. Okay – you've told me. I don't know what the hell you expect me to do. I don't know what the bloody blazes anybody can do. You've spewed it out of your conscience. Fine! That's your limit of positive action. Once you get the pus out of a boil it heals. So – start healing. Come and see me in five years and I'll take you out to dinner."

Then he smiled.

Zanny didn't smile back, but she felt the cage of her frustration bending a little. Her mind had stopped converting pence into shillings. Her hands had stopped battering on unyielding doors. His door had opened a little. His disbelief had been dented. They had communicated. There was a tiny little glow under her naval where his hands had touched.

"Just one pill?" she heard Mummy uttering in disappointment.

"Packs one hell of a punch," Caradoc lied.

"I thought that – perhaps – for myself – ?" Clare suggested tentatively.

"Oh," asked Caradoc, "what's your crime then, – arson?"

Clare stalked out in silence. "An impossible man," she told Graham. "No wonder his practice is dwindling. Have you noticed how plebeian the doctors are these days? He should be on a footplate of a train heaving coal."

"Not smooth like Tolliston, you mean," said Zanny, getting back into the car.

It was a tactless remark and she knew it. On the whole, she was feeling better. Had Murphy prodded her in her naval it would have felt the same. Firm very masculine fingers. But the soil got embedded in yours, Murphy, and you hadn't the time to wash.

I'm aching for you. Sighing for you. Tonight we'll sit it out together in our minds. What you suffer, I'll suffer. I'll be with you every step of the way.

She refused to take Caradoc's pill.

Clare, annoyed and tired of the whole business, said "Stew, then!" and walked out of the bedroom.

Graham, more loving, more patient, less sensitive, less guilty, crushed it up and put it in her hot chocolate. "Cross my heart," he said, "there's no pill in this."

"Then give me Ovaltine."

"We're out of it," he lied, "darling, please."

Because she loved him, she took it.

He bent and kissed her and smoothed her hair away from her forehead. It would never happen again, he believed. She had suffered too much this time. She would never kill again.

Murphy's suffering he dropped a veil over in his mind. To help the veil stay down he intended to drink as heavily as he dared. Clare would drink with him. Would Murphy drink, he wondered? Would they allow him to pickle his mind in alcohol so that in the end everything was a complete and merciful haze?

Don't think.

Don't think.

Don't think.

At two o'clock in the morning Clare went and sat in the hall with the telephone receiver cradled on her knee. She hadn't yet made the call to the police station, but when her voice was steady enough she would make it. The last few hours of deliberate imbibing hadn't taken the edge off anything – in fact the booze had made her feel worse. A small draught from the hall window made the glass pendants of the chandelier jangle softly against each other in what seemed to her agonised conflict. Graham, who hadn't gone to bed either, was on his way upstairs to the lavatory when he saw her sitting there. He asked her mildly what she was doing. She told him: nothing – yet.

He changed his route and made for the kitchen.

When he returned he was carrying a pair of kitchen scissors.

She asked, "You're going to cut it?"

"Yes."

She didn't make even a token protest, but held up the telephone cord and tried to stop thinking about Murphy's rope.

"I've got to tell them," she said, still holding the cord taut and very handy.

"But now you can't," he said comfortingly, and snipped it.

She began to weep softly with relief.

"Silly cow," he said gently, "silly, maternal, stupid cow. Let's hope she's sleeping."

Zanny was.

Caradoc's magic had nothing to do with his wonder pill. He was with her in her dreams. They were transported back in time to the sinking of the *Titanic*. The band was playing "Abide with Me". Old Granny Morton was leading the singing. Mournful, toothless, and with a voice like a sick crow she stood on a rostrum and skinny-armed conducted the damp passengers in their final song. Zanny, wet to her knees, and with tears pouring down her cheeks, raised her voice with the rest. And then, miraculously, Caradoc was beside her. "Let's get the hell out," he said.

Up on deck the sun shone. The sea, a long way down, was an acid green. "Now, bloody jump!" said Caradoc.

His arm was around her waist and they floated down through lavender smoke as the *Titanic* tilted sideways.

They were together on a raft on a shipless sea. The sea went on for eternity, gentle and blue and beautiful. She had nothing on. "Damn and blast," he said, poking her stomach, "but you're beautiful."

"So are you," she whispered, "so are you." There was something familiar about the naked male body – a little niggle of pain came and went. Out of the cloudless sky came a single drop of rain. It dropped into her navel and turned into a small, perfect, creamy pearl. She touched it wonderingly and then she touched him. The waves began to suck and flow – suck and flow – in a wonderful rhythm. She moaned gently.

Graham and Clare, pausing by the bedroom door, heard the moan and interpreted it very decently as sorrow and remorse. That their interpretation could well be off-beam they realised with some surprise. Bitch, Clare thought. The life force, Graham thought. He suggested to Clare that they should go to bed. Destruction and creation – it was a fine balance. A life went out – a new life came in. Drunkenly philosophic he went to great lengths to explain to Clare why he wouldn't wear his sheath. But she was past caring.

"Odd that the telephone should be dead," said Sergeant Thomas, aiming the car up into the hills. "Under the circumstances, probably just as well," said Detective Inspector Warrilow. It was a nice morning. The mountains were clear of cloud. The air was very clean. "You'll leave most of this to me," he reminded Thomas. "None of your Welsh . . . what's the word . . . *hwyl?*" Slightly offended, Thomas didn't answer. He couldn't see how religious ecstasy equated with what lay ahead. He wished he could turn the car around and go back home. Sausages for breakfast. Tea the colour of soft brown leather, thick with sugar. Warrilow, as lean as Cassius, was breakfastless, too. Vulpine, Thomas thought. In the thick undergrowth of your mind lurks your juicy prey. A morning of blood – this. Not nice.

Graham was shaving when he saw the police car coming up the drive. It was nine o'clock. Murphy had been dead an hour. At eight o'clock he and Clare had turned their backs on each other and pretended to be asleep. She had been shivering under the bed-clothes. He had gone down and made her a cup of tea. He had made one for Zanny, too, but fortunately she was still asleep. There was a tiny little smile on her lips and her cheeks were flushed.

As he looked out of the bathroom window now he was reminded of that other awful morning nine years ago. It was a small fat Zanny in those days with a bow in her hair. Ferret-sharp little Dolly. Two different policemen. Nowadays, a posher, bigger car. Had they come to say that Murphy had been hanged? Surely not. It would be an unusual courtesy. Courtesy? (Was he still drunk?) It would be in the papers soon. On the wireless. He went in to alert Clare.

"You'd better get dressed."

"I feel sick."

Her lips were dry and flaking and her skin seemed to be drawn too tightly over her cheek-bones.

"You'll be better when you've freshened up," he told her. It was trite, but true. Ablutions didn't wash away guilt, but you felt slightly more normal afterwards.

She looked at him with bitter enmity and swung her legs over the side of the bed. Why were the police here now? Would she have time to have a bath? Why did life keep ticking on? Why couldn't one take a huge chunk of it and bury it somewhere deep and dark? She wished she were sixty and on the threshold of senility. If Graham had made her pregnant during the night she would abort it.

The bell rang.

"Nice garden," said Thomas to Warrilow, making conversation. Warrilow didn't answer. Given encouragement Thomas would start complimenting Moncrief on his chrysanthemums and write down details of his favourite fertiliser. He could hear Moncrief coming across the hall. When he opened the door he bade him a polite good morning, and introduced himself and Thomas.

"You have heard," he said, "that Murphy has been reprieved?"

Quite obviously Moncrief hadn't. His reaction, Warrilow observed, was distinctly out of proportion to the news. He reacted like a relative. He didn't know what to do with himself. A few steps back into the hall. A fiddling with the brass gong on the hall table. (For a moment Warrilow thought he was going to beat it.) A few steps up the stairs – and then down again. "Do please go into the sitting-room and pour yourselves a drink." Followed by: "I must tell my wife – and good Christ – Zanny!"

Warrilow was abrupt. "Not for a moment, sir."

But Clare, at the top of the stairs, had heard. She was in her dressing-gown and her feet were bare. She came down the stairs softly as if not quite sure where the steps were. She sat on the bottom step and began to cry. Graham sat beside her. "Bit of a shock," he said.

"So I see," Warrilow observed dryly. "I wasn't aware you were acquainted with the man."

Graham and Clare, like two punch-drunk fighters in a ring, heard the warning bell for a new round and struggled out of their corners to face whatever came next. Surely nothing came next? This was it. Victory for Murphy. Victory for life over death. Amen. Draw down your own personal curtain. You've lived through a horror that didn't happen. You've been battered and beaten and bloody and bowed – now pick up your towel and go home. Tonight you'll sleep. In the meantime there are two policemen over there looking very curiously at you. The sitting-room door is open and the room is dusty and untidy. There's half a bottle of scotch

183

on the table and empty glasses. There's a cushion on the floor and yesterday's newspaper.

Yesterday, Murphy, you faced death. You shouldn't have faced it. Even if you had committed the crime the death penalty should have been commuted long ago. Well – the reformists had argued it that way. Thin, circumstantial evidence. Nothing solid to go on.

"So," said Clare, becoming calm again, "the judges in the appeal court saw sense?" (But they hadn't – had they? At this late stage it would be the Home Secretary – wouldn't it? Why wasn't Warrilow answering?)

She got up and led the way into the sitting-room. "It was very good of you to come and tell us." She picked up the cushion, smoothed it, and put it on the sofa.

"You would have phoned, I suppose," Graham conjectured, "had the phone been working?"

Warrilow, who had already noticed the cut wire, didn't comment on it. He and Thomas sat on a couple of chairs in the window recess. That this was a repetition of a scene from the past he wasn't to know. The room was chintzy – cosy. He was aware that Thomas had settled back comfortably against the cushions.

"Pretty little gel," Thomas remarked, noticing the photograph of ten-year-old Zanny on the piano. She wore her hair in two plaits then and her eyes gazed into the middle distance.

Warrilow scowled at him.

"It now seems perfectly possible," Warrilow said, "that Murphy didn't murder Bridget O'Hare."

He watched Clare and Graham for their reaction. They were seated side by side on the sofa and were facing the window. They had themselves in hand. They were cool. The mother's eyes had narrowed slightly as if she were defending the pupils from close scrutiny. Emotional reaction showed in the pupils. She wouldn't know that, probably. The father had reached over to the box on the small brass table for a cigarette and then the fingers had seemed to forget temporarily what they were searching for. He had touched air before the brain messages activated the fingers again.

"Cigarette, Inspector?"

Warrilow declined.

"Sergeant?"

Thomas, who would have liked one, refused. He felt like a deacon in the big seat under the eye of a hell-fire minister. All he would be allowed would be an occasional amen while Warrilow rent the air. A quiet hell-raiser, Warrilow – a whispered amen.

"You mean," Graham suggested, "that the O'Hare girl's death was accidental?"

"I had no intention of implying that," Warrilow answered.

"Then . . .?"

"I should like to break the news of Murphy's reprieve to your daughter," Warrilow said. "I believe she's on the premises?"

"Yes, asleep in bed." (What in hell are you getting at? This is no joyous breaking of good news.)

"Then could you perhaps give her a shout from the hall? Tell her she is wanted downstairs."

Graham, busily erecting staves of protection around his threatened young, was about to burst out into a furious tirade against police methods when Clare stopped him.

"Of course you want to break the good news," she said silkily. "It must have amused you very much when Zanny took the blame on herself. It's good of you to take the time to bother." She looked at Graham in warning. He drew shakily on his cigarette and was silent.

Zanny was at a tea-dance with Caradoc when she heard her mother calling. Her dress was of bright blue satin with white bows on the shoulder. "Blasted pretty dress," he was saying, "but prettier without." They were on their honeymoon in Greece. "Damn fine place for a honeymoon," he had told her. And it was. Very hot sand. Very hot Greek food. Very hot love-making in the little white villa on the seashore. "Blasted interruption," said Caradoc inside her head. She was coming awake slowly, her body warm and lethargic. Mummy was shouting in the hall.

So breakfast was ready.

Well – she was hungry for it.

It was strange that she had known Doctor Caradoc for such a short time and felt that she knew him so well. She had a vague idea that there was a Mrs. Caradoc who ran a riding school. A rough, tough, horsy, female, probably. Perhaps that was where he had learnt to swear so much. Not that she minded. Riding schools were dangerous places. Horses ran amok. Trampled people. If a horse ran amok in a confined space – like a stable – the chances of getting out alive were remote. Horses were excitable creatures. It would take very little to make them excited. It might be possible during the holidays to ask Daddy if she might take riding lessons. It would be very interesting to get to know Mrs. Caradoc. Mrs. Caradoc would ask her over to the house. In time the strained relationship between the doctor and his wife would become clear. "My dear child," Caradoc would say to her, "you see how it is. You're a bloody comfort to me – do you know that?" Their hands would touch in silent understanding.

Zanny began to dress.

She put on the first dress that came to hand – a green cotton one. Her school shoes didn't go with it, but it didn't matter. After breakfast she'd take a walk into the village. Surgery would probably be over by then and he would be out on his rounds. She wondered what kind of car he'd have. Nothing too smooth. He might offer to give her a lift.

She washed perfunctorily and ran a comb through her hair. It was a lovely day. There was sun everywhere.

The shadows began to crawl around her when she walked into the hall. There was no smell of bacon. There

186

were strangers in the sitting-room. Not strangers. She knew one of them. Thomas from the local police.

Thomas?

Murphy?

The hall clock struck the half-hour of nine. He had been dead one and a half hours and she hadn't given him a single thought. Stricken, she walked into the room.

A small, thin man, with a lot of dark hair and eyes like Daddy's razor blades, was standing up and coming over to her. He was telling her that Murphy wasn't dead. *Murphy was reprieved.* How terribly nice of him! What awfully good news! The sun was out again in a great big burst of yellow.

"By God!" Zanny said, startling everyone. "What bloodily, awfully, splendid news!"

She sat down on the nearest chair and grinned widely at them all.

"A reprieve," Warrilow said, recovering himself, "doesn't mean that Murphy walks out a free man. It means that instead of being hanged, he will spend the rest of his life in prison."

"While there's life," Zanny said, "there's hope."

They had been set an exercise once on clichés. It was desirable, apparently, to learn them. As white as snow. As black as coal. As white and shiny and gorgeous as our future together, Caradoc. And nothing awfully black and terrible happening to Murphy. I'm not fickle. Not really. I was awfully fond of him for quite a long time. It was just when you touched me last night . . . he'd never touched me. Now the last thing I want in the world is for him to touch me. You're very clean. I like the way you smell. I think that night in the cottage he must have been drunk. I didn't want to admit it then, but I do now. After all, the truth is the truth. And I didn't much like his not having all his teeth. I pretended I didn't mind. But I think I did, really. You have to learn by going from man to man. Only I think I'll stop with you. I'm sure I'll stop with you. Dinner in five years, you said. Don't be silly, Caradoc. In five years I'll be twenty. I'm not going to throw all that time away. We've got now – now – now!

Not a flicker of guilt, Warrilow thought. Psychotic.

Like a little flower opening in the sun, Thomas put it. Pity there's evil at the heart of it.

Oh, God – Doctor Caradoc, Clare thought, recognising the language.

The real you, Zanny, Graham willed, is the way I see you now. Happy. With a grin on you like a Cheshire cat. Wish I could take you on my knee. Wish I could boot these policemen to hell. Wish none of it had happened.

"If you should see Murphy in prison," Zanny told Thomas, "would you give him my very best wishes and tell him how pleased I am?"

"Yes, indeed," said Thomas, "with pleasure." He felt as if he walked in some fey countryside where the craziest remarks made sense.

Warrilow's countryside was very rational. He trod his route with precision, perfectly sure of where he was going.

"Do you think Murphy murdered Bridget O'Hare, Susannah?" he asked.

"Zanny," Zanny corrected him. "I think she might have fallen," she said cautiously.

"In your statement to Sergeant Thomas you said that you had murdered Bridget O'Hare."

"Just a bit of nonsense," said Zanny. "Miss Sheldon-Smythe went around the convent saying the same thing."

"Miss Sheldon-Smythe was in town having her hair permed at the vital time," Warrilow said. (A casual remark dropped by Constable Jones, the husband of the hairdresser, had produced this bit of evidence – though it hadn't been considered important. Miss Sheldon-Smythe hadn't been under suspicion – any more than this girl had been.)

"I was picking flowers," Zanny said, "and most of the time I was with my friends. Anyone will tell you that. I didn't push Bridget O'Hare."

"But you kept on insisting that you did."

"Only to save his life."

Warrilow smiled thinly. "That was very noble of you. Why should you want to do that?"

Zanny blushed. "Well – I rather liked him."

"If you still rather like him, then the prospect of his serving a long prison sentence must rather disturb you?"

"I really am awfully sorry for him," Zanny said, shifting uncomfortably, "but I don't see what I can do."

(Murphy, I'm sorry. But today is different from yesterday. Today there is Caradoc. And tomorrow there is Caradoc. You're yesterday, Murphy. You've gone.)

Warrilow turned to Graham and Clare. "Your daughter's confession of guilt seemed very unlikely at the time," he said. "Had you backed it, however, it would have been believed."

"It was crazy nonsense, as the child's just told you," Clare expostulated.

"Utter rubbish," Graham agreed.

"You were placed in an extremely difficult position," Warrilow went on unperturbed. "Maybe that is why you cut the telephone wire on what you thought was Murphy's last night?" It was small actions, such as that, that indicated complicity. They knew – had known for a long time – he was sure of it. His own certainty had grown during the last twelve hours. He had been wrong about Murphy. He had begun to doubt his guilt during the trial. The mentality to murder was the x factor that balanced the equation. In this case an elusive x factor – until now.

"I caught it in the Hoover," Clare said. "The cord snapped."

"When one's own kith and kin are concerned," Warrilow continued smoothly, "one tends to ignore the ethics of a situation. In certain circumstances it's almost forgivable – almost, but not quite."

"If we're talking about ethics," Graham snapped, "shouldn't we apply them to police procedure? Is this an accusation? Is it an inquisition? You've made no formal warning. Should I contact my lawyer?"

Warrilow acknowledged the criticism, but refused to be deflected. If his route were circuitous – and it was – he had good reason. "You will, no doubt," he said, "contact your lawyer in time. If a charge were to be laid against you, it would be one of criminal negligence. A lethal virus needs to be contained."

Graham's forgotten cigarette was burning up into his fingers. He flung it in the ashtray. "I don't understand you. Are you accusing my daughter of murdering Bridget O'Hare?"

Warrilow sat back in his chair. All his movements were relaxed and leisurely. "Well, Susannah," he said, "do you think I might be?"

She had no doubt at all that he was. So there had been a witness then? Someone on the run from the police, perhaps, who hadn't come forward until the last minute? An army deserter, maybe?

"Witnesses lie," she said. "If you've got a witness, then he's telling lies."

She held Warrilow's gaze. His words were sharp little points of pain in her eyeballs, but she refused to lower the lids. Her hands in her lap were loose and relaxed.

For sheer cold-blooded nerve, he thought.

"Witness?" Graham's voice grated with tension. "Are you trying to tell us there's a witness? I've never heard such goddamned nonsense! Look at her . . . are you trying to say that she's capable of hurting anyone . . . that she went up on the headland . . . that she and Bridget . . .? My God, I think you're mad . . . why the hell have you come here? To tell us that Murphy has been reprieved because my daughter . . . because Zanny . . . because someone has framed my daughter, Zanny . . ."

190

He was becoming incoherent with rage and terror.

Warrilow was reminded of a jungle family of lions, the male snarling vengeance as the hunters closed in.

Your daughter is a vicious little feline, he thought. She's not even cowering behind you. She's out in front – as cool as dammit.

Of course the case would be difficult to prove. Almost impossible. It was on the cards that no one would try to prove it, though he'd push it all he could. Certainly there wouldn't be another confession from little Miss Moncrief. After a passionate urge to tell the truth she was now swinging the other way. He wondered why.

It was time to answer her father's questions – so he answered them.

"Your daughter might or might not have murdered Bridget O'Hare," he said. "She might or might not have been telling the truth when she stated that she did. She might or might not be telling the truth now when she says that she didn't. There were no witnesses. Murphy was reprieved – not because there was any additional evidence – but because in murders of this kind, which are not pre-meditated, the death penalty is not always carried out."

Graham's face was puce. Relief and anger fused into an explosive mixture that made his heart thump so hard he thought he was going to be sick. He had been led down tortuous evil paths by a twisted police officer. He had been played with. Dangerous admissions might have been milked out of him by reptilian methods. Might have been milked out of Zanny. She'd had the good sense to deny everything. Warrilow would suffer for this. He would complain to his superiors. He would have him demoted. He had acted outside the law. He had no business to be here at all.

Warrilow, who had a fair idea of what was going through his mind, gave him a moment or two to calm himself. He looked at the girl's mother. She was very pale and contained. Her long slender fingers were pulling little bits of fluff off her dressing-gown. She looked like a patient who had just been given a reasonable prognosis. And now she was going to be slammed back under the surgeon's knife.

At times like this he didn't like his job very much. But it had to be done.

He turned back to Zanny.

"You pushed it down the back of the radiator, didn't you?" he said to her. "And I suppose your school uniform is hidden away somewhere?"

Zanny didn't answer. He was being rather too quick for her. She needed time. The non-existent witness had just faded off into the salty sea air of the headland. She had just turned smiling to Caradoc and told him that all was well. And now they were back in the convent again. They were back to yesterday evening. Events that seemed to belong to a dim and distant past were coming back.

"Not that we need your school uniform," Warrilow went on. "The shoes you're wearing now are evidence enough." He indicated the stains on the black leather. "Blood, of course."

"If you say so," said Zanny politely.

"Oh, you don't have to take my word for it," Warrilow was equally polite. "She didn't die until five o'clock this morning. She might not have died at all had she been discovered earlier. She was able to speak to us and we have her statement. A blackboard compass, wasn't it? According to her she'd drawn a circle with it – with figures one to twelve – a clock, perhaps?"

"Not really," said Zanny. "The twelve times table – one o'clock was one shilling, and so on. She made me repeat it ten times."

"And then?"

"And then she fell on the compass. The sharp end. It stuck in her throat."

"A great pity," said Thomas, jerked out of his silence.

"Well, she was being rather a nuisance," Zanny said

mildly, "and she did get rather on my nerves. Sister Clemence was a very intense nun – not very well balanced, if you know what I mean."

There was silence for several minutes. The curtains moved softly in the breeze and the scent of autumn wood smoke drifted in.

"She said she'd pray for you," said Thomas. "Those were her last words." Like a little angel on a tombstone you are, he thought, with the breath of life breathed into you – more's the pity. Little angel of death.

Mother Benedicta would pray for her, too, Zanny was quite sure. All this praying was a bit of a bore. Sister Clemence dying was an incredible bit of bad luck, though at the time she had hoped with some passion that she would. It was a pity that she hadn't died *at once* – before she could talk. Like the others. She hadn't included her in the confession she had made to Caradoc. She hadn't been dead when she'd left her and a wounding had seemed too trivial to mention. Besides, she hadn't attacked her on Murphy's account. Unlike Bridget and the judge Sister Clemence had nothing to do with him. She had jabbed her with the compass before she could stop herself – or think of the consequences. It was as simple as that. Caradoc's five years might still prove true after all. He would come and visit her in prison. They would reach out and touch each other's hands through the grille. Her prison dress would be grey with a white collar. Her hair, cut short, would curl into the nape of her neck. Her cheek-bones – high and dramatic like Garbo's – would accentuate the deep glowing blue of her eyes. She would be pale and interesting and terribly beautiful – and mature. She would look at least nineteen. He would tell her how much he loved her. "Bloody hell," he would say, "my body burns for you." His wife, in the meantime would have a fatal fall from a horse – unaided. Or she would meet someone else and there would be a divorce. It would be quite all right in the end. Nothing particularly unpleasant would happen to her. It never had. Why should it now?

Why was Mummy shivering and moaning on the sofa?

And why was Daddy looking at her like that?

"It will only be a few Hail Marys," she told them cheerfully, "and I've always found the police awfully nice."

"Good," said Warrilow softly, standing up. "Then perhaps you wouldn't mind accompanying us?"

"Not at all," said Zanny.

Then she smiled at him. Brilliantly.